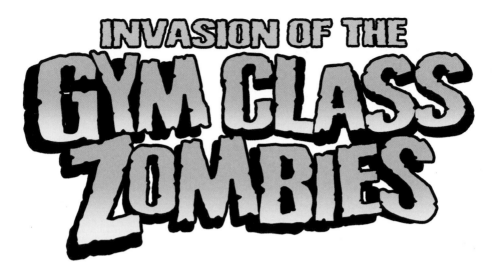

INVASION OF THE GYM CLASS ZOMBIES

Librarian Reviewer
Katharine Kan
Graphic novel reviewer and Library Consultant, Panama City, FL
MLS in Library and Information Studies, University of Hawaii at
Manoa, HI

Reading Consultant
Elizabeth Stedem
Educator/Consultant, Colorado Springs, CO
MA in Elementary Education, University of Denver, CO

STONE ARCH BOOKS
MINNEAPOLIS   SAN DIEGO

Graphic Sparks are published by Stone Arch Books
151 Good Counsel Drive, P.O. Box 669
Mankato, Minnesota 56002
www.stonearchbooks.com

Library of Congress Cataloging-in-Publication Data
Nickel, Scott.
    Invasion of the Gym Class Zombies / by Scott Nickel; illustrated by Matt Luxich.
    p. cm. — (Graphic Sparks—School Zombies)
    ISBN 978-1-4342-0453-0 (library binding)
    ISBN 978-1-4342-0503-2 (paperback)
    1. Graphic novels. I. Luxich, Matt. II. Title.
PN6727.N544I58 2008
741.5'973—dc22   2007031252

Summary: With the evil scientist Dr. Brainium in jail, Trevor thought his zombie-busting
days were over. Then his new teacher, Mr. Brawnium, turned the whole gym class into
radio-controlled jocks! Can Trevor save his zombified classmates from this muscle-bound
madman? Or will he be trapped in dodgeball doom forever?

Art Director: Heather Kindseth
Graphic Designer: Brann Garvey

1 2 3 4 5 6 13 12 11 10 09 08

Printed in the United States of America

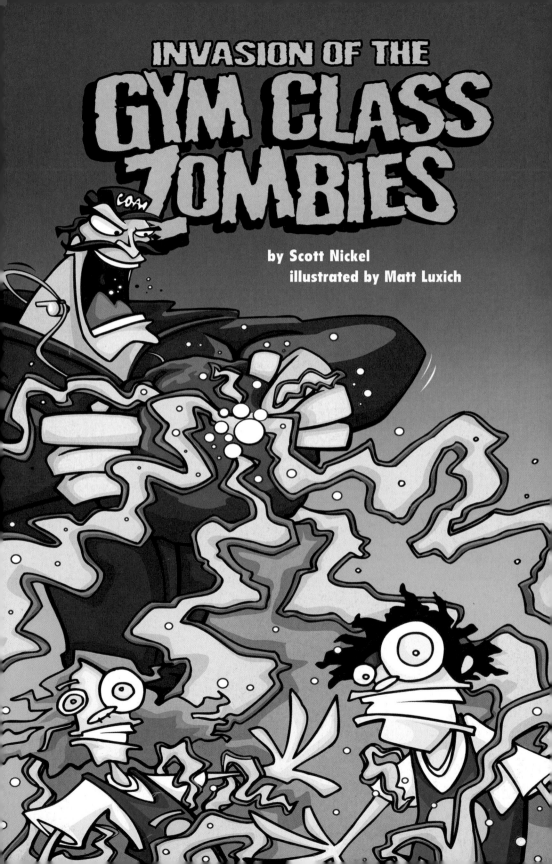

INVASION OF THE GYM CLASS ZOMBIES

by Scott Nickel

illustrated by Matt Luxich

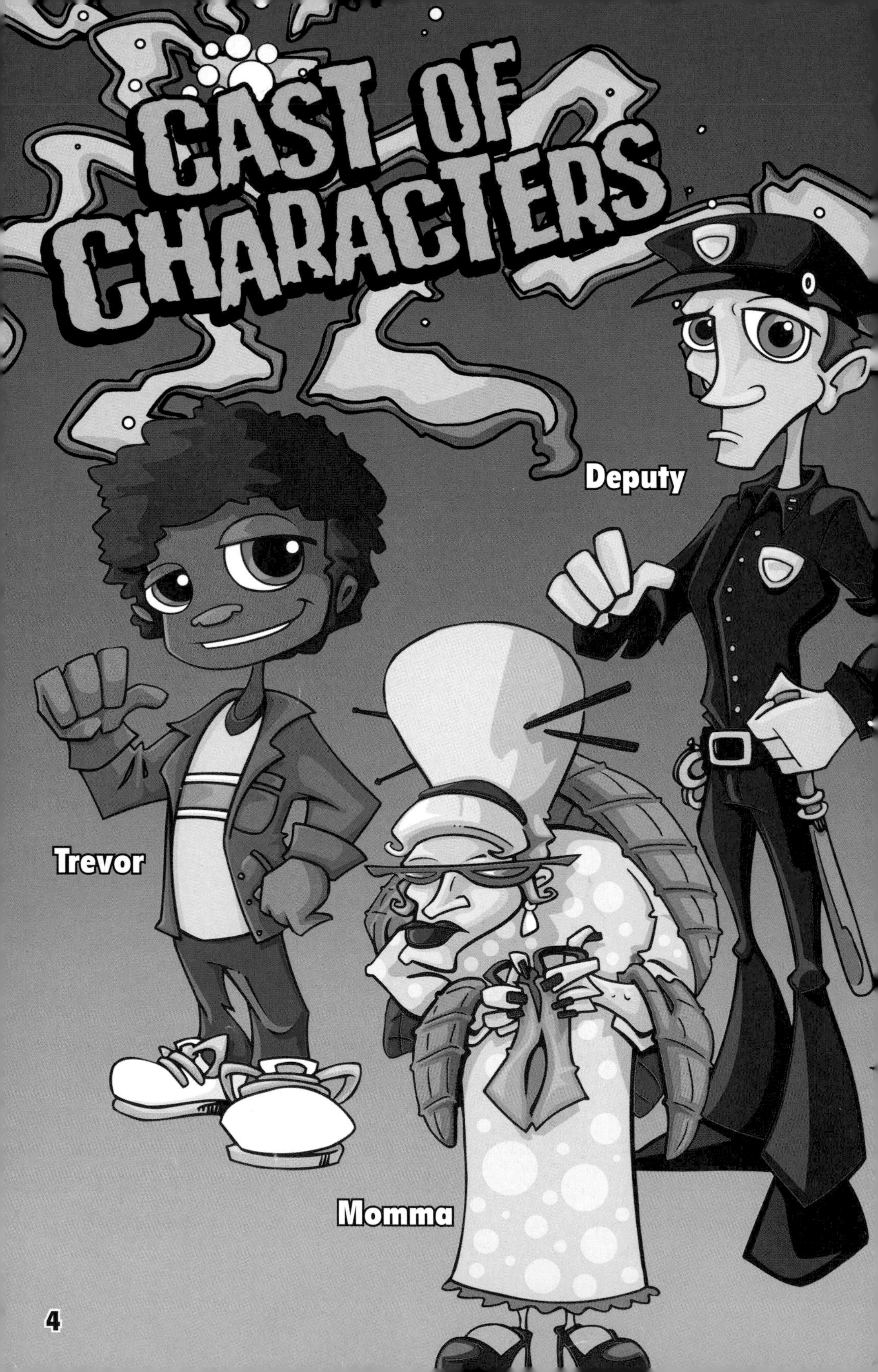
CAST OF CHARACTERS
Deputy
Trevor
Momma

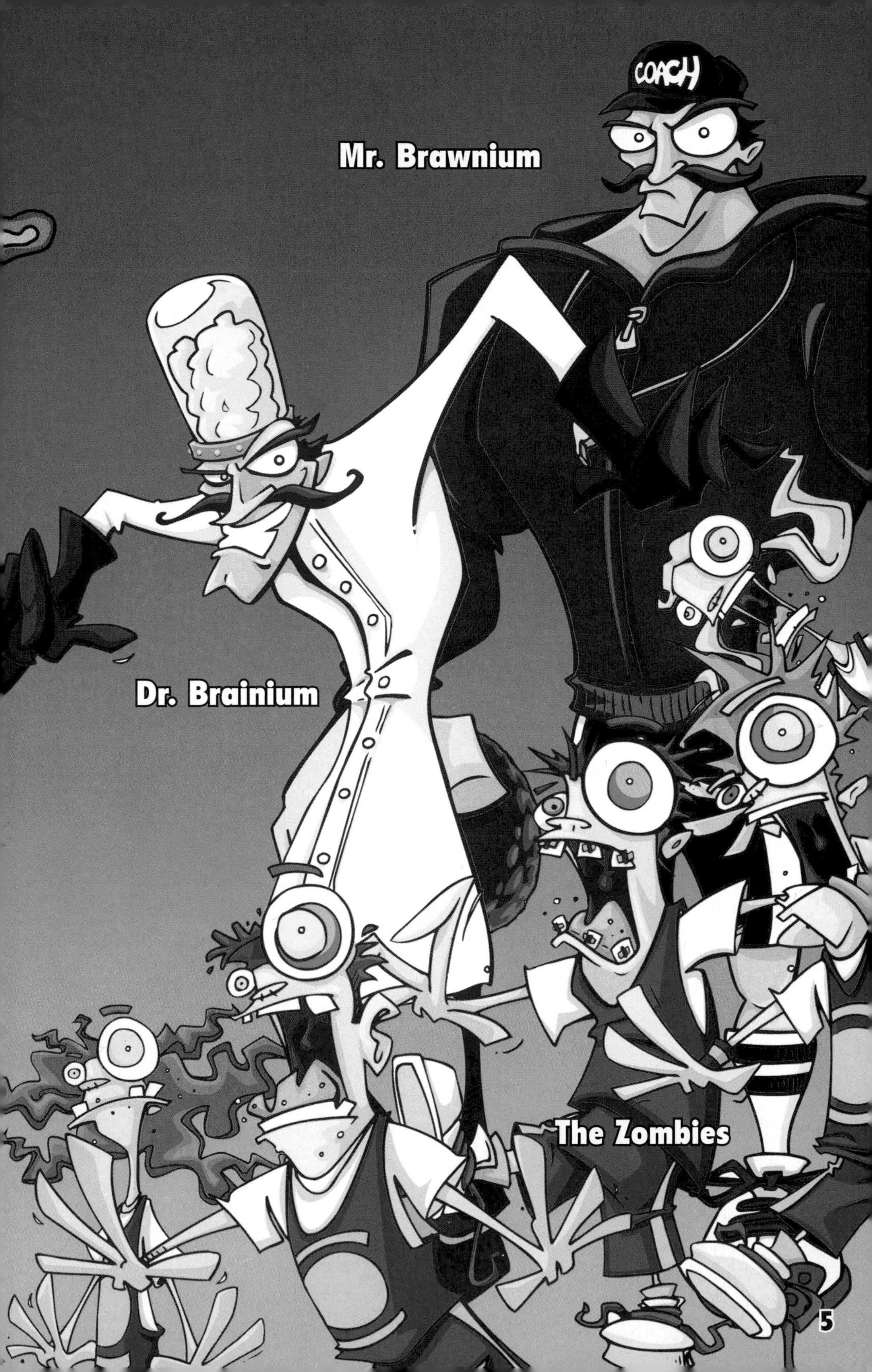
COACH
Mr. Brawnium
Dr. Brainium
The Zombies

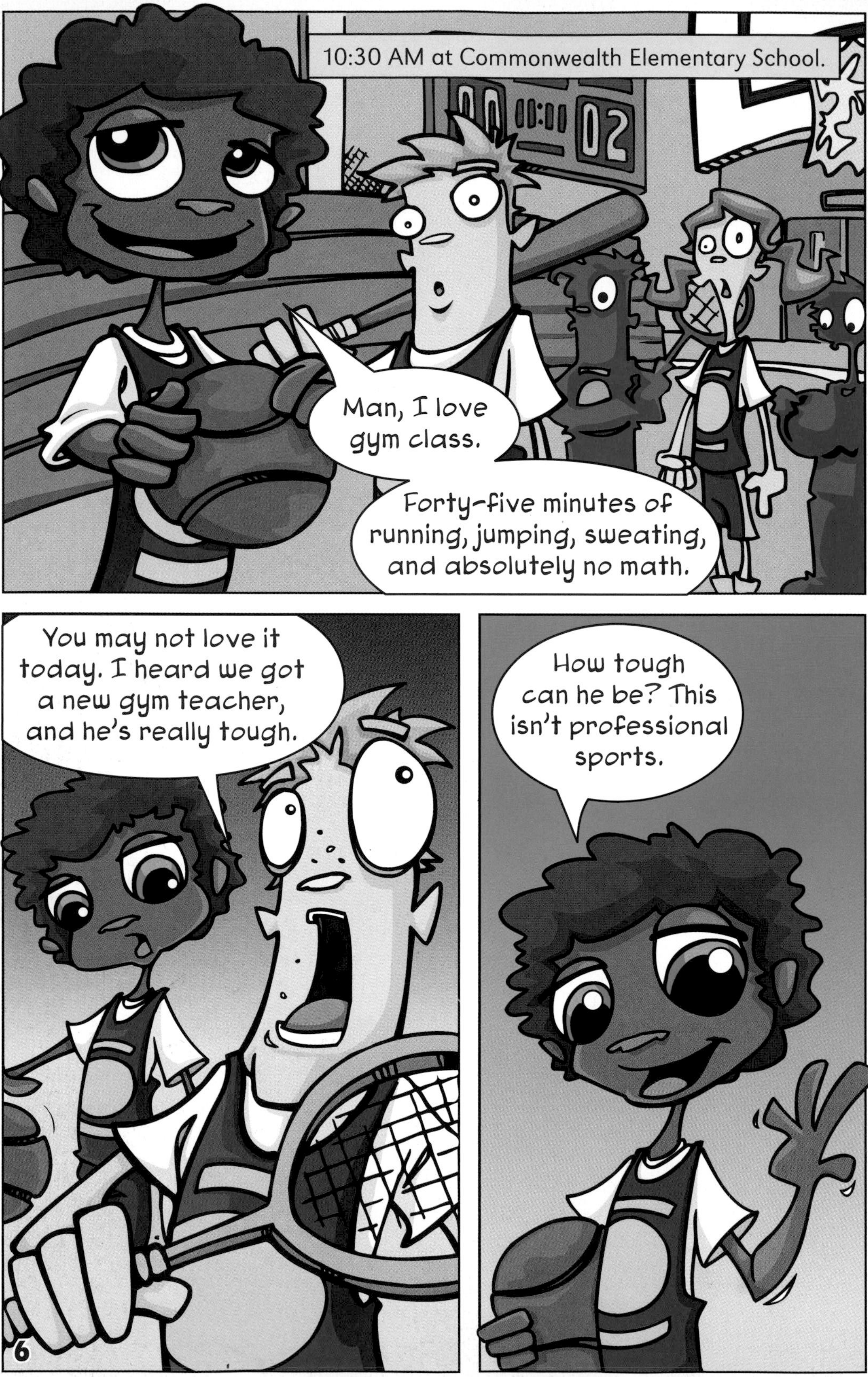
10:30 AM at Commonwealth Elementary School.
Man, I love gym class.
Forty-five minutes of running, jumping, sweating, and absolutely no math.
You may not love it today. I heard we got a new gym teacher, and he's really tough.
How tough can he be? This isn't professional sports.

Quiet down!!
COACH
I'm Mr. Brawnium, here to turn you little babies into rough, tough athletes!
We'll start out with 50 push-ups and 50 sit-ups. No whining!

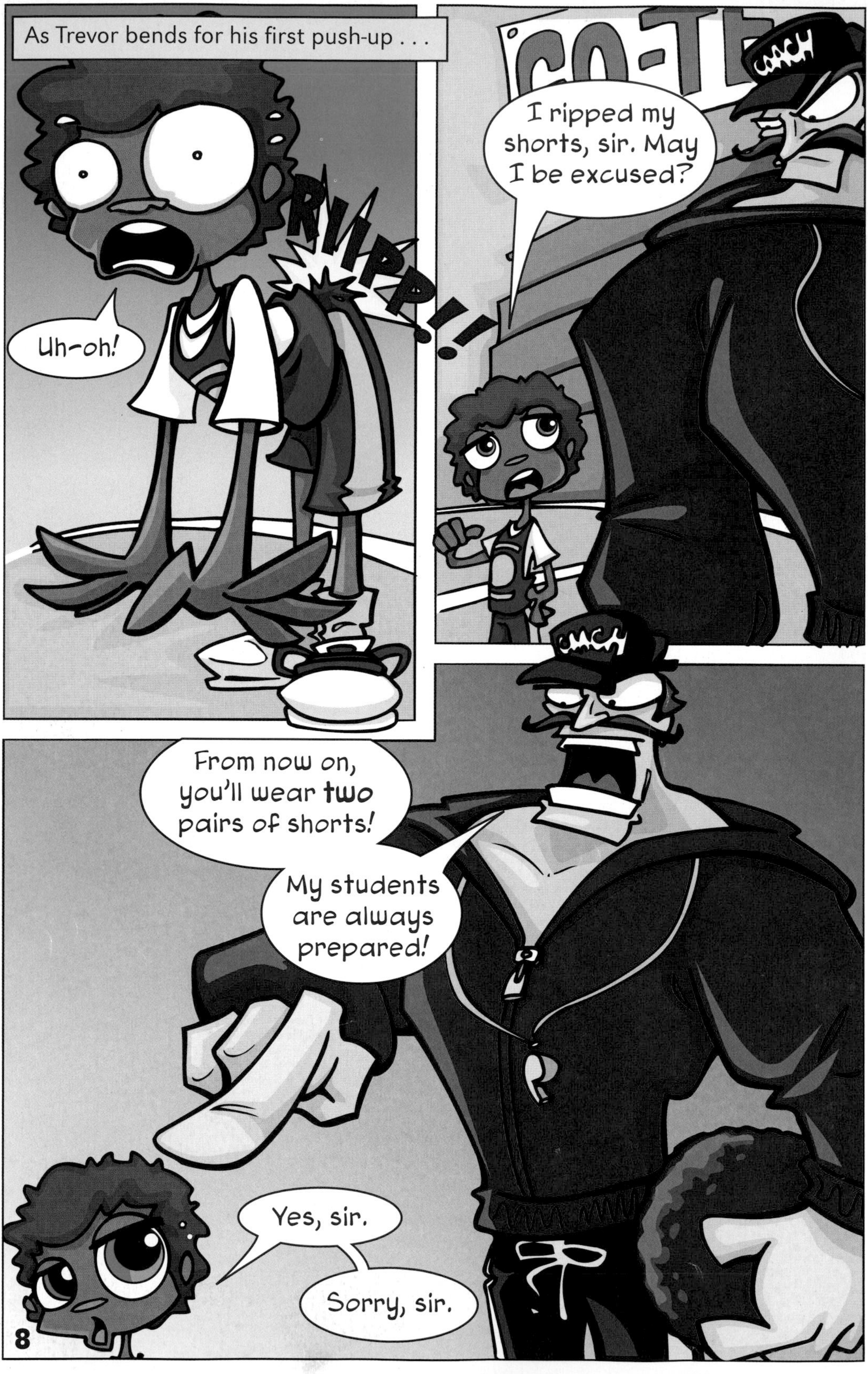
As Trevor bends for his first push-up . . .
RIIIPP!!!
Uh-oh!
I ripped my shorts, sir. May I be excused?
COACH
From now on, you'll wear **two** pairs of shorts!
My students are always prepared!
COACH
Yes, sir.
Sorry, sir.

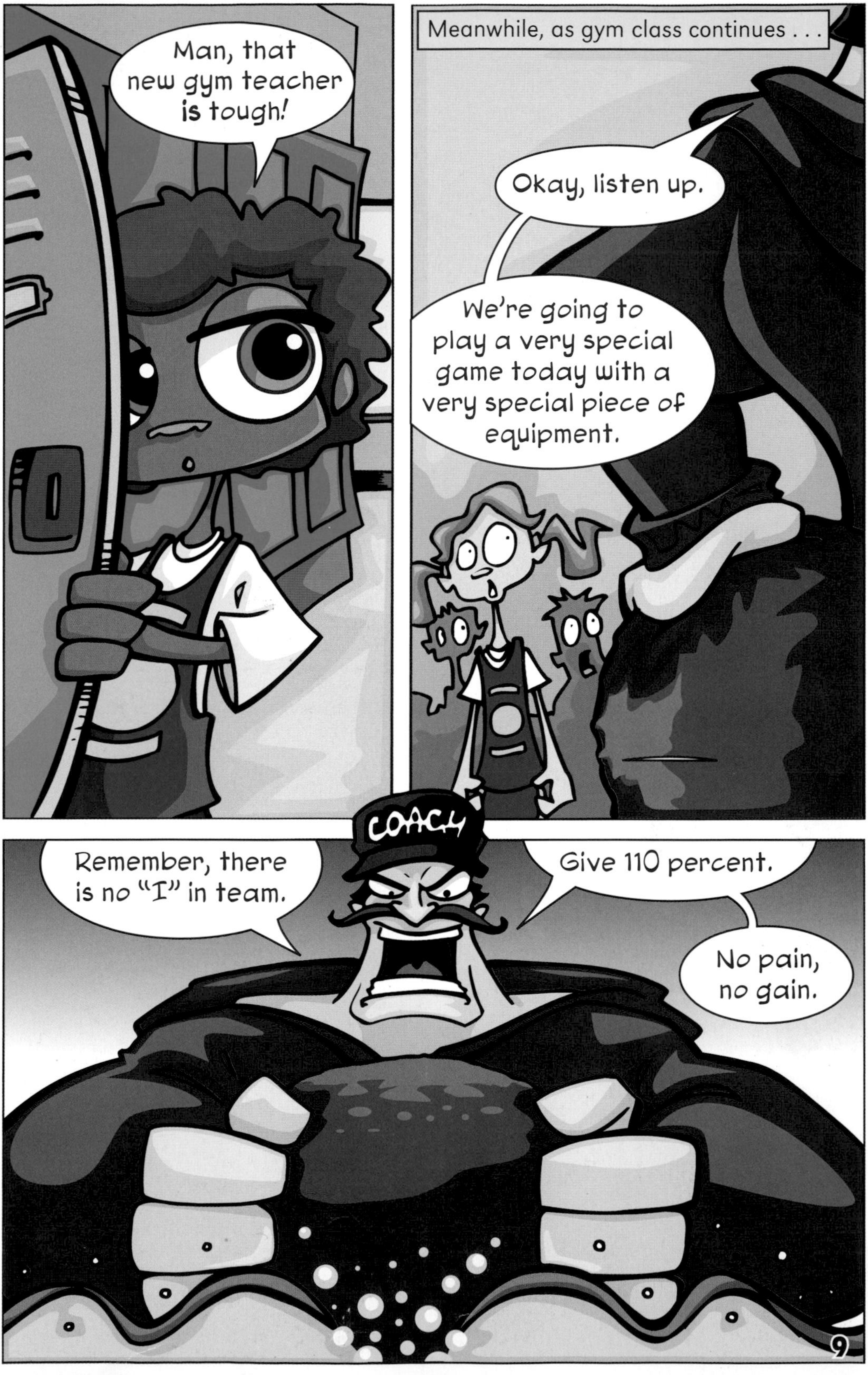
Man, that new gym teacher is tough!
Meanwhile, as gym class continues . . .
Okay, listen up.
We're going to play a very special game today with a very special piece of equipment.
COACH
Remember, there is no "I" in team.
Give 110 percent.
No pain, no gain.

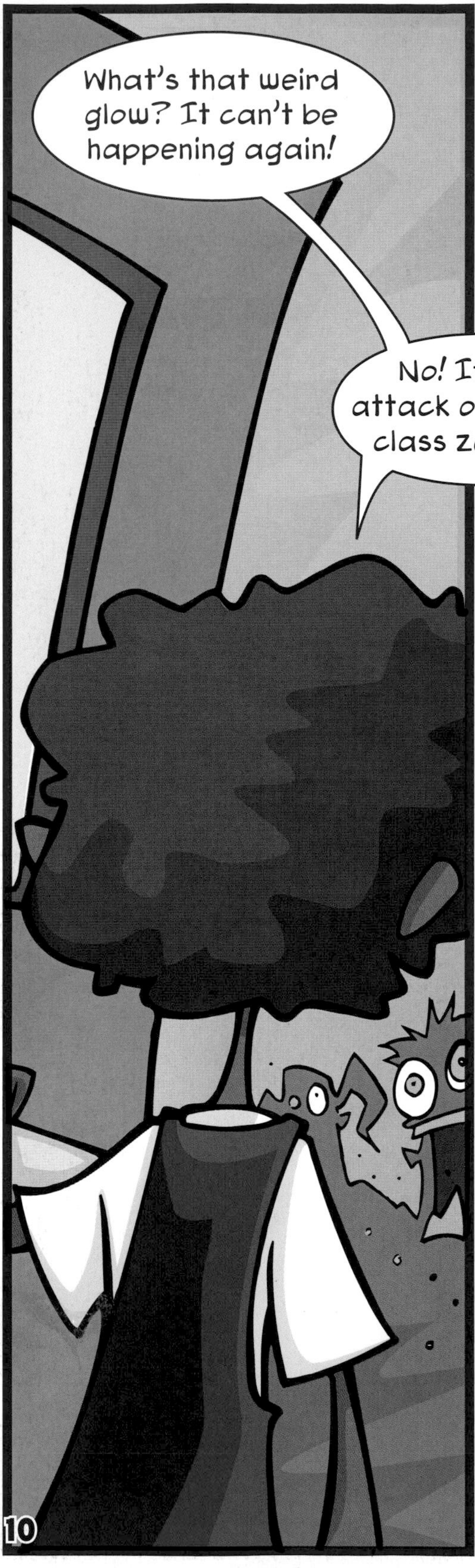
What's that weird glow? It can't be happening again!

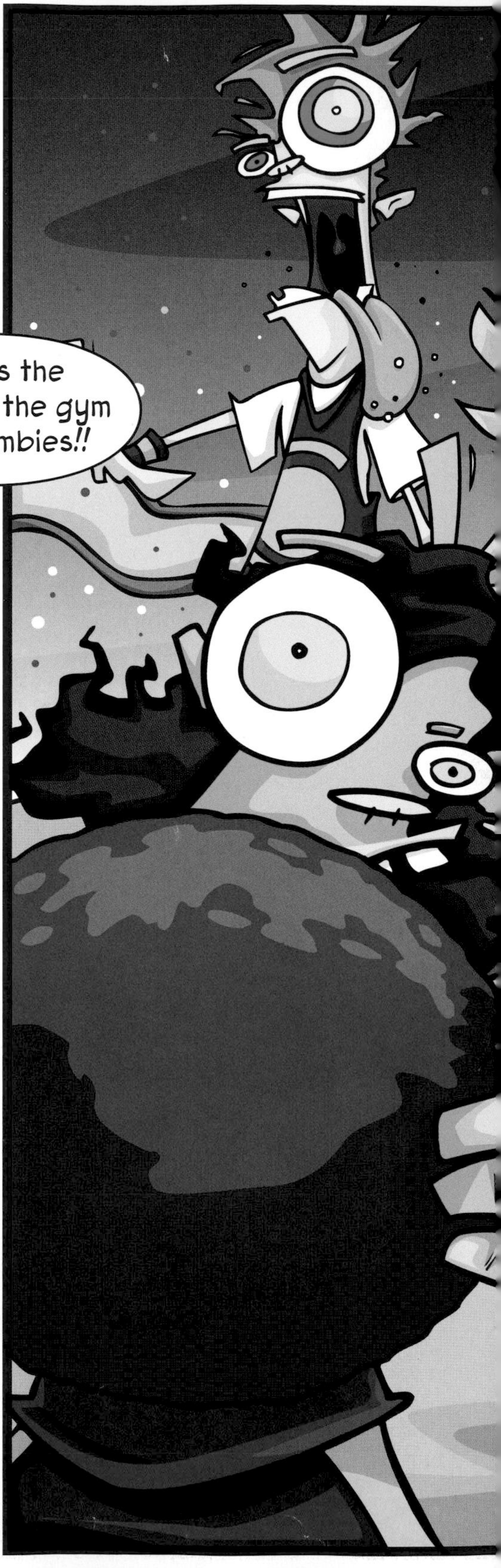
No! It's the attack of the gym class zombies!!

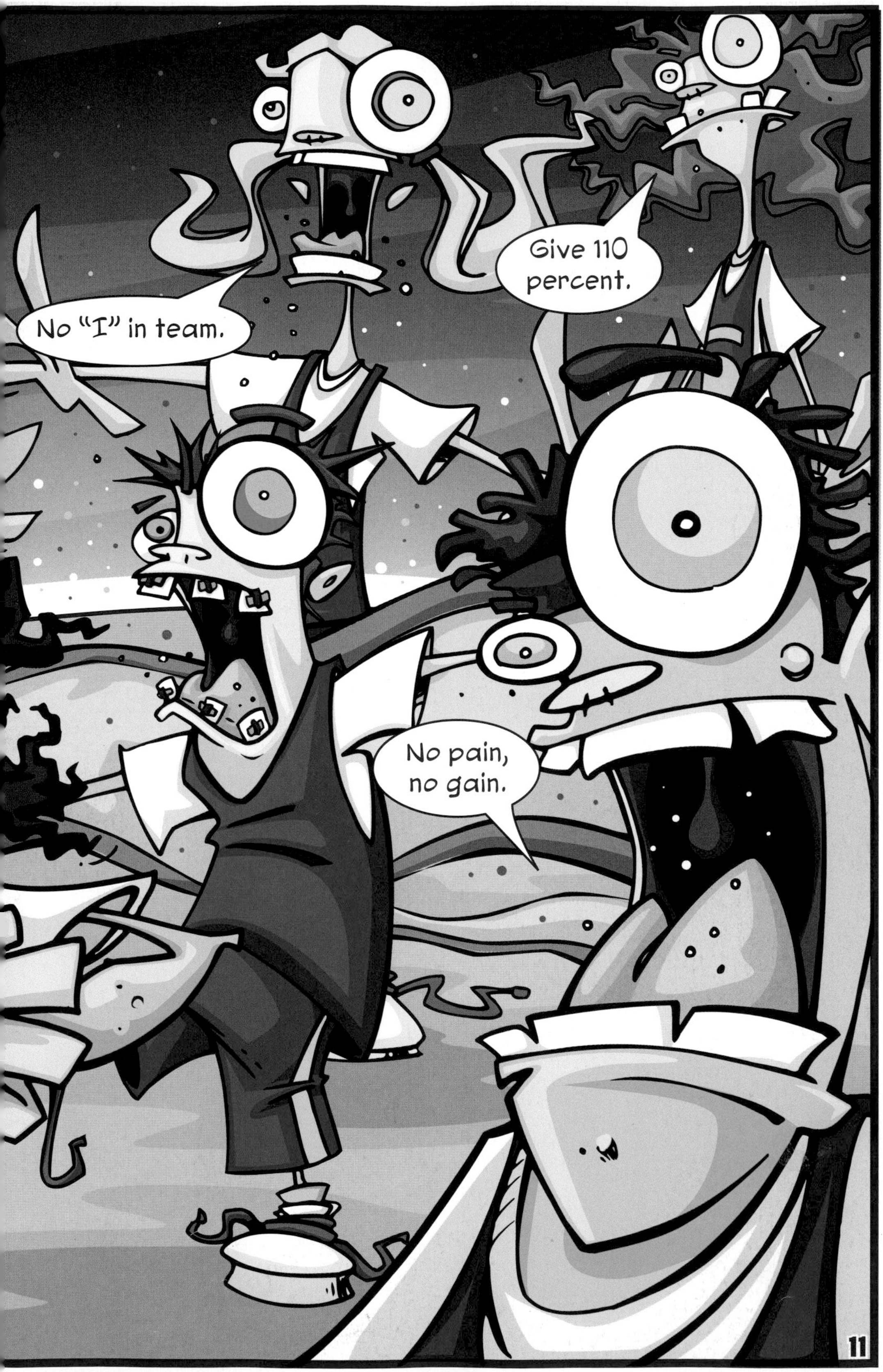
Give 110 percent.
No "I" in team.
No pain, no gain.

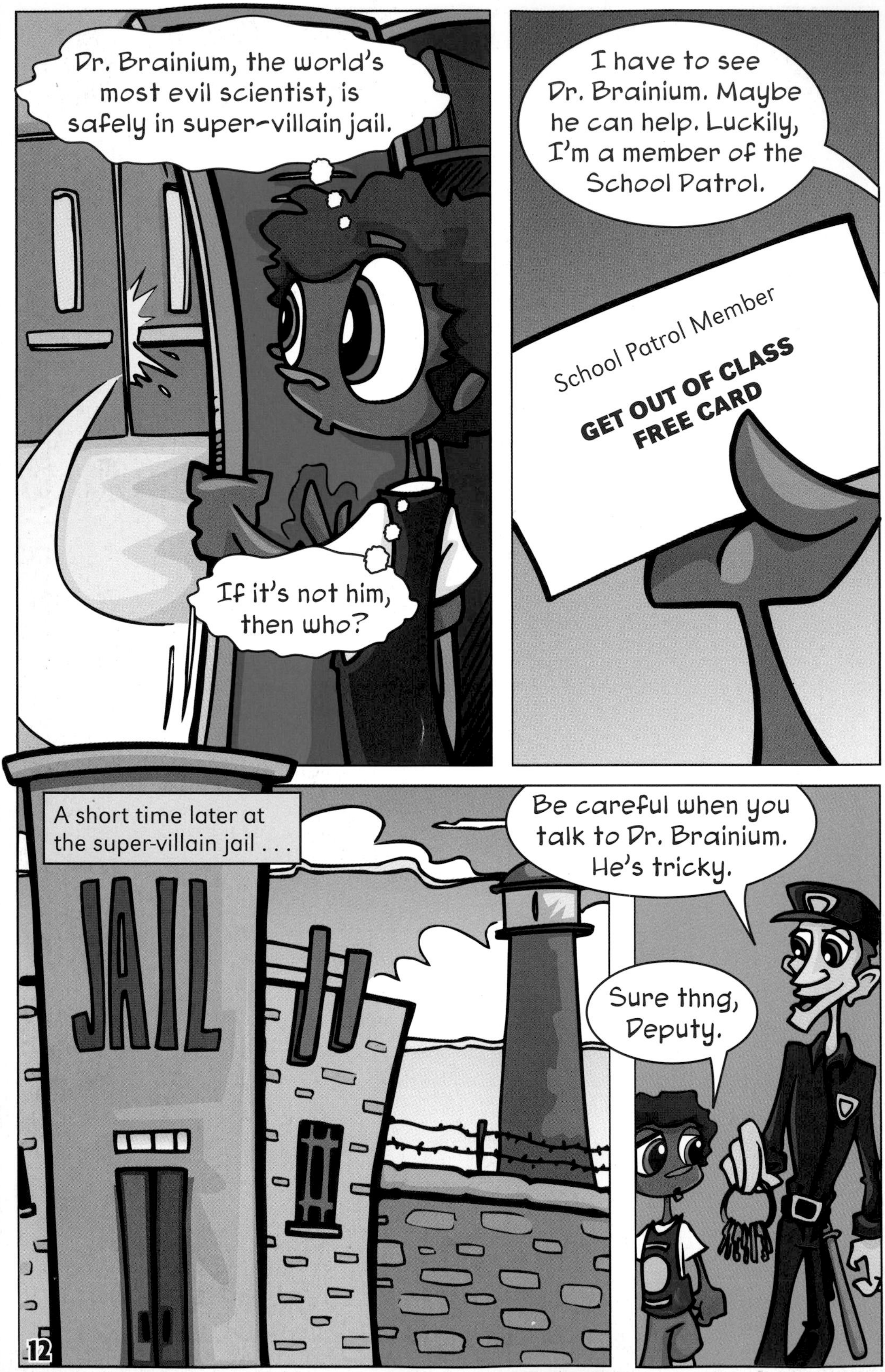
Dr. Brainium, the world's most evil scientist, is safely in super-villain jail.
If it's not him, then who?
I have to see Dr. Brainium. Maybe he can help. Luckily, I'm a member of the School Patrol.
School Patrol Member
GET OUT OF CLASS FREE CARD
A short time later at the super-villain jail . . .
JAIL
Be careful when you talk to Dr. Brainium. He's tricky.
Sure thng, Deputy.

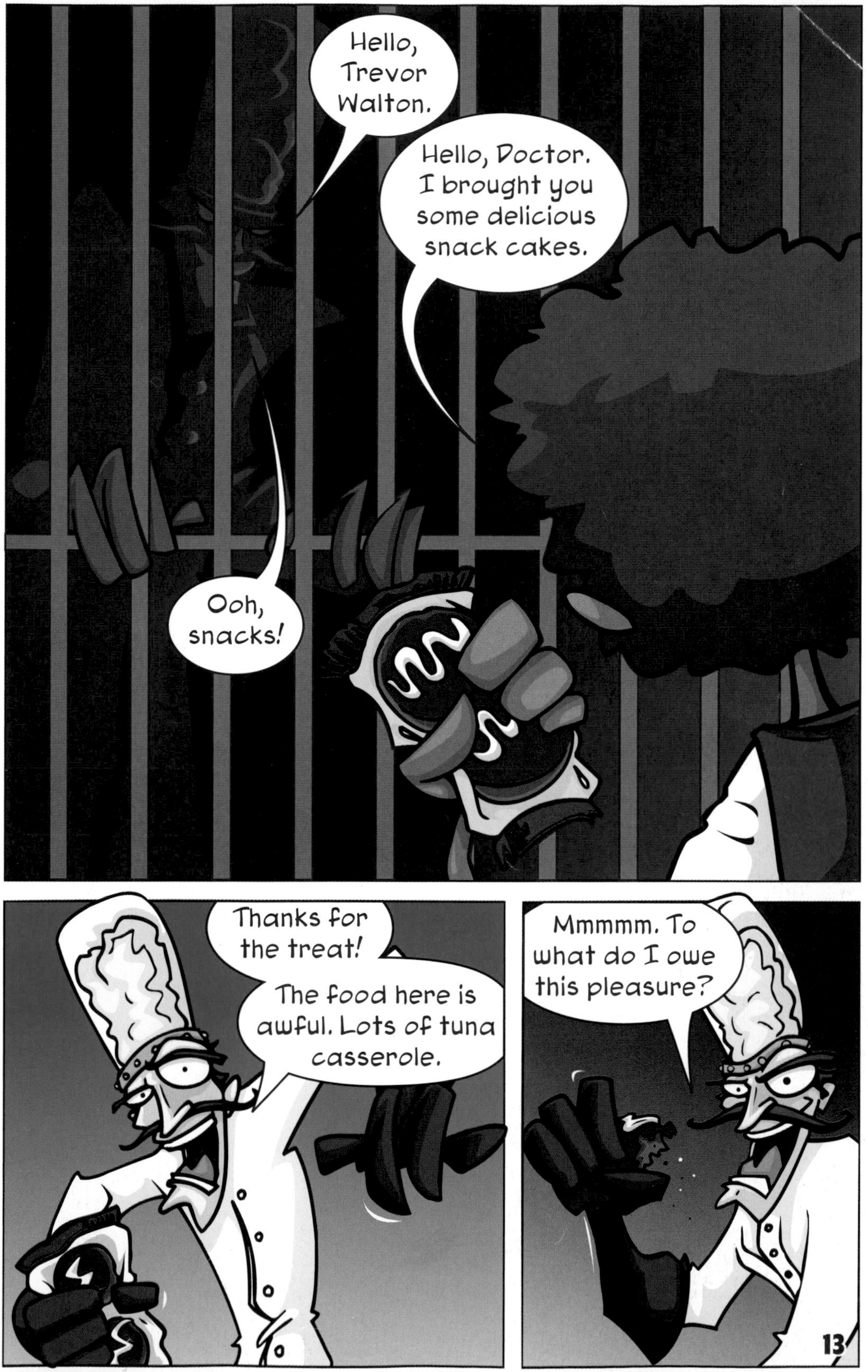
Hello, Trevor Walton.
Hello, Doctor. I brought you some delicious snack cakes.
Ooh, snacks!
Thanks for the treat!
The food here is awful. Lots of tuna casserole.
Mmmmm. To what do I owe this pleasure?

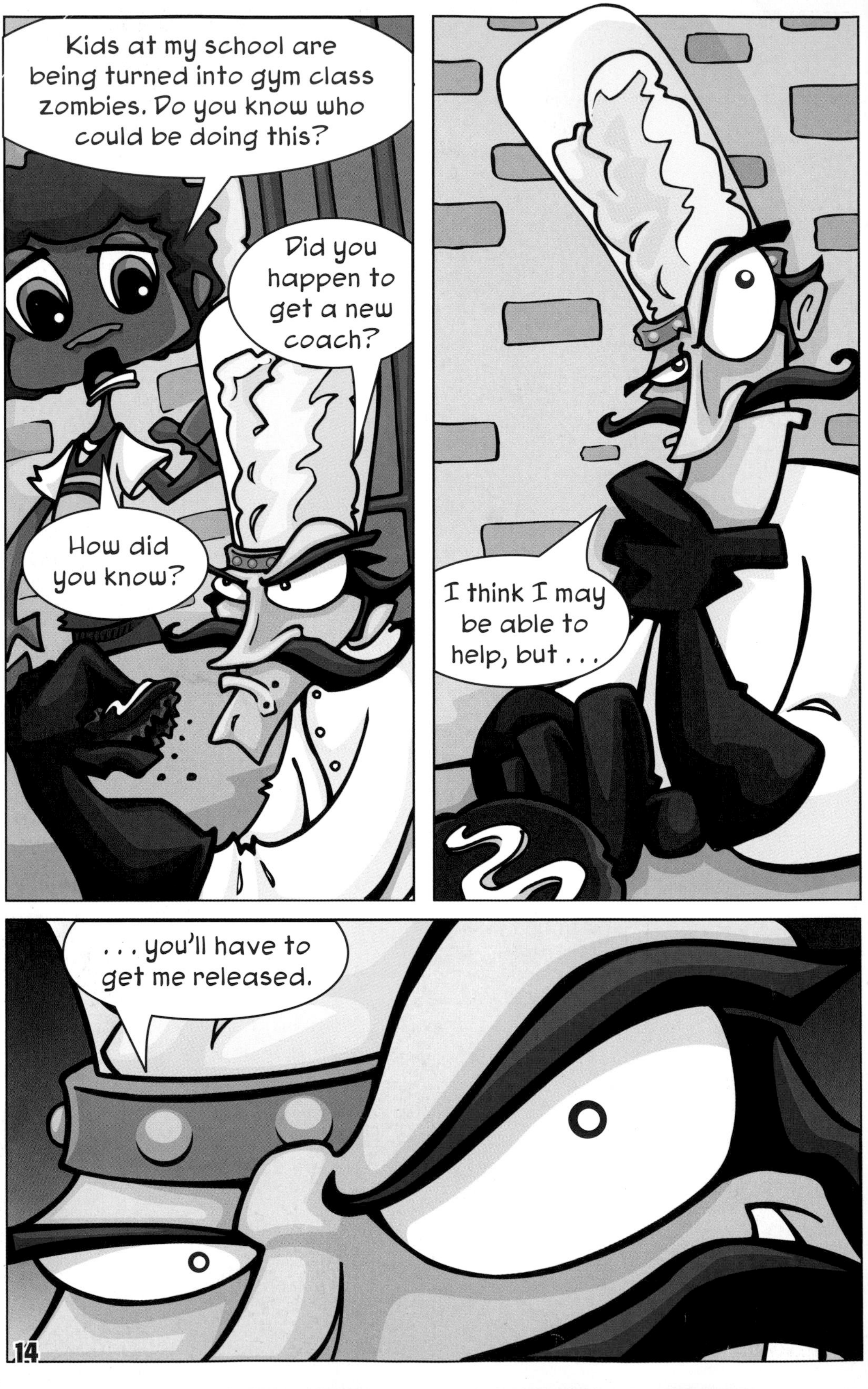
Kids at my school are being turned into gym class zombies. Do you know who could be doing this?
Did you happen to get a new coach?
How did you know?
I think I may be able to help, but . . .
. . . you'll have to get me released.

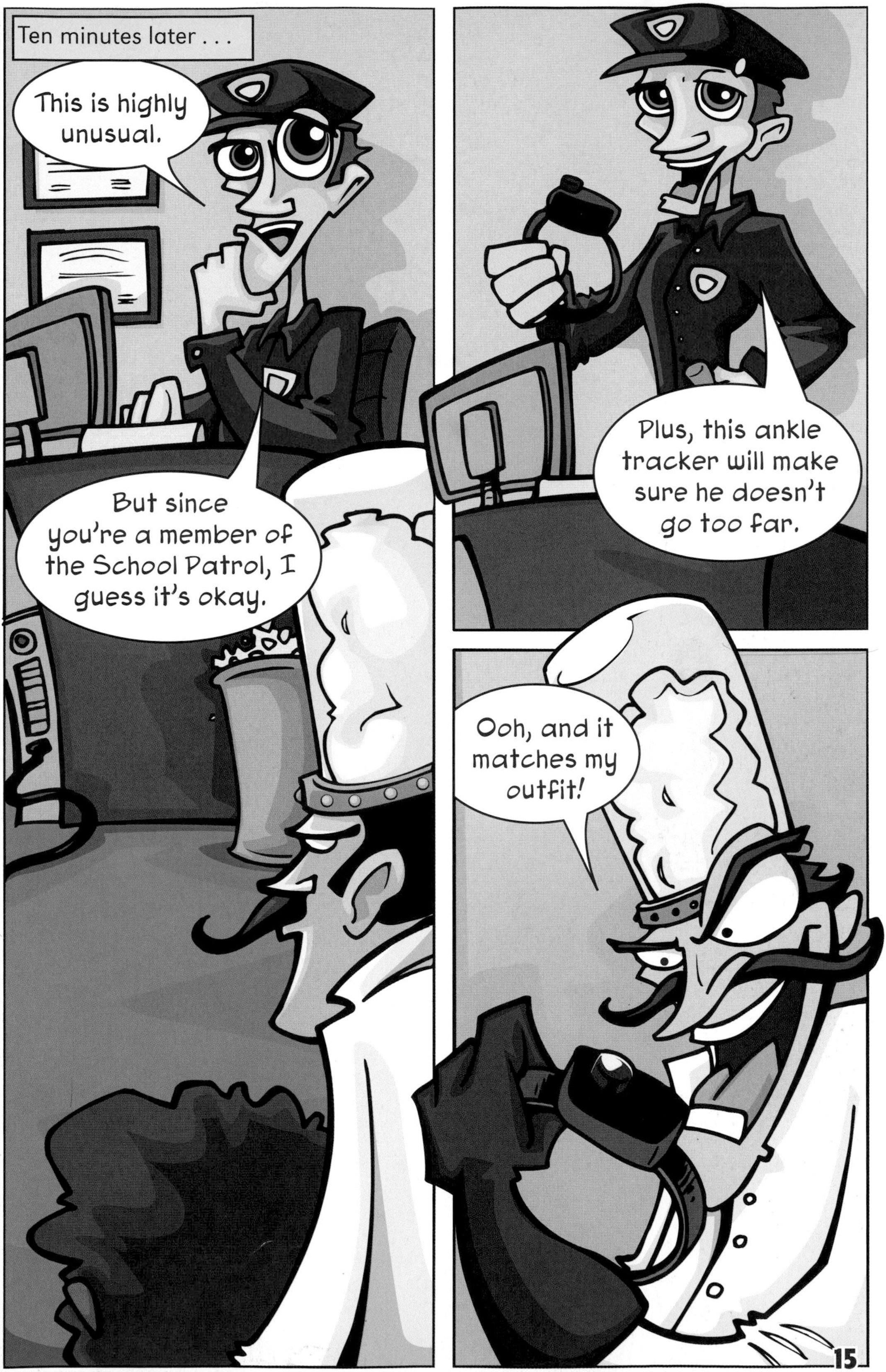
Ten minutes later . . .
This is highly unusual.
But since you're a member of the School Patrol, I guess it's okay.
Plus, this ankle tracker will make sure he doesn't go too far.
Ooh, and it matches my outfit!

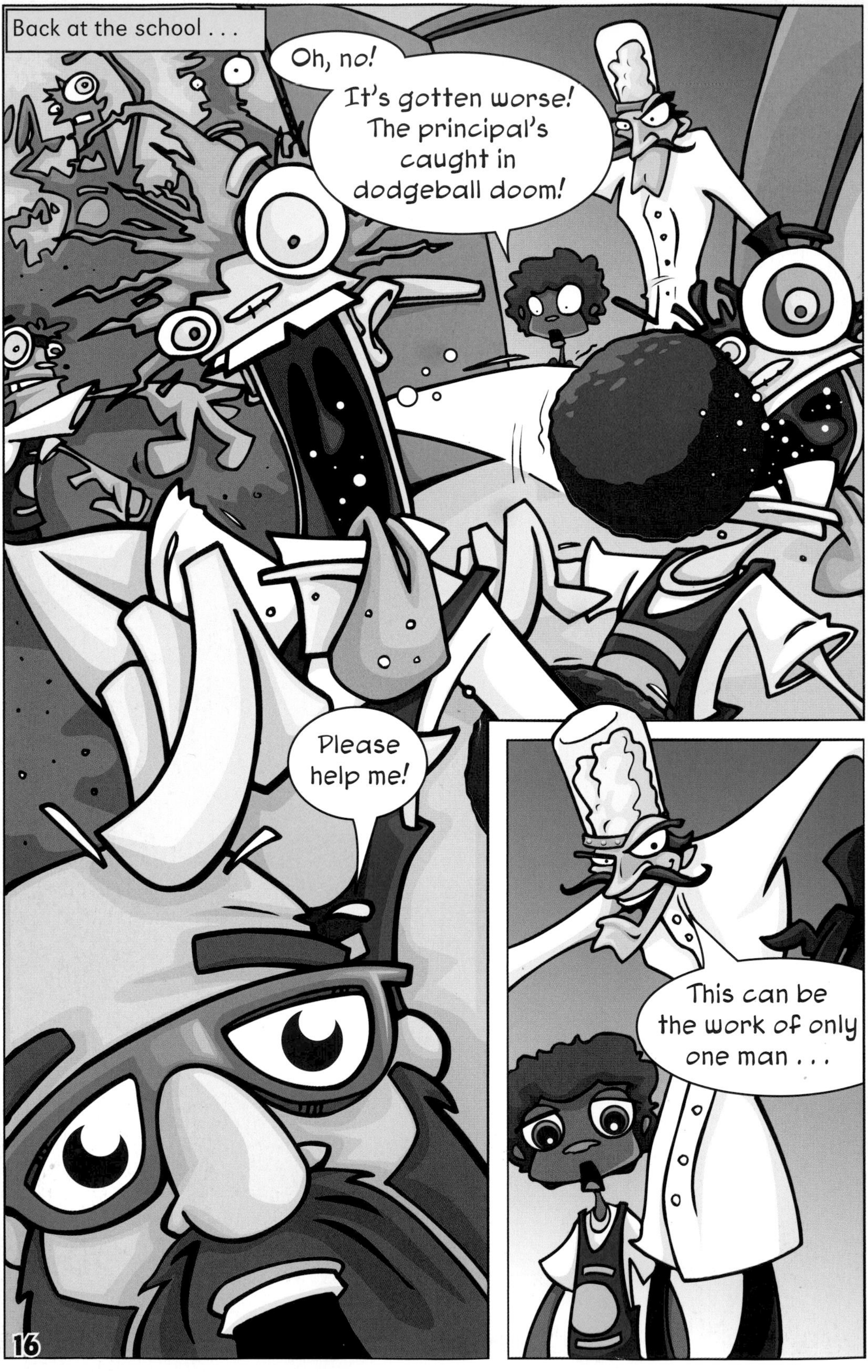
Back at the school . . .
Oh, no!
It's gotten worse! The principal's caught in dodgeball doom!
Please help me!
This can be the work of only one man . . .

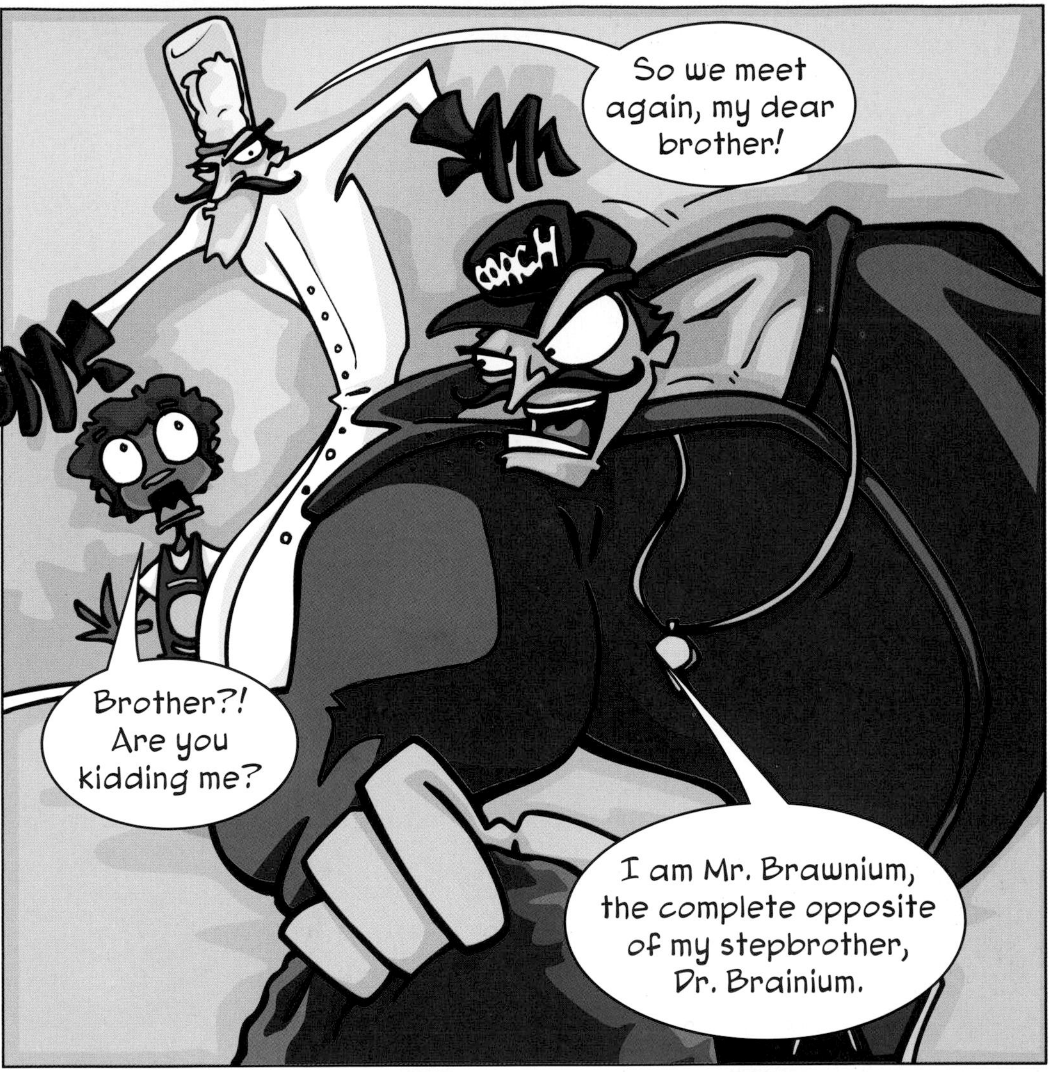
So we meet again, my dear brother!
COACH
Brother?! Are you kidding me?
I am Mr. Brawnium, the complete opposite of my stepbrother, Dr. Brainium.

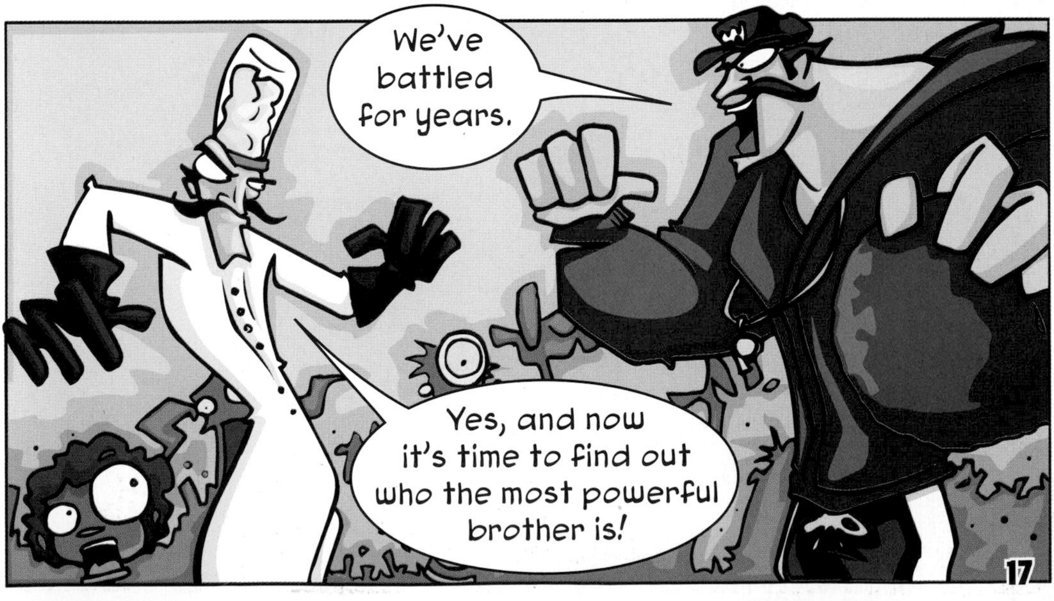
We've battled for years.
Yes, and now it's time to find out who the most powerful brother is!

COA
You and all your books and fancy education.
Learning drools and sports rule!
TSSSSSSSSSSS!

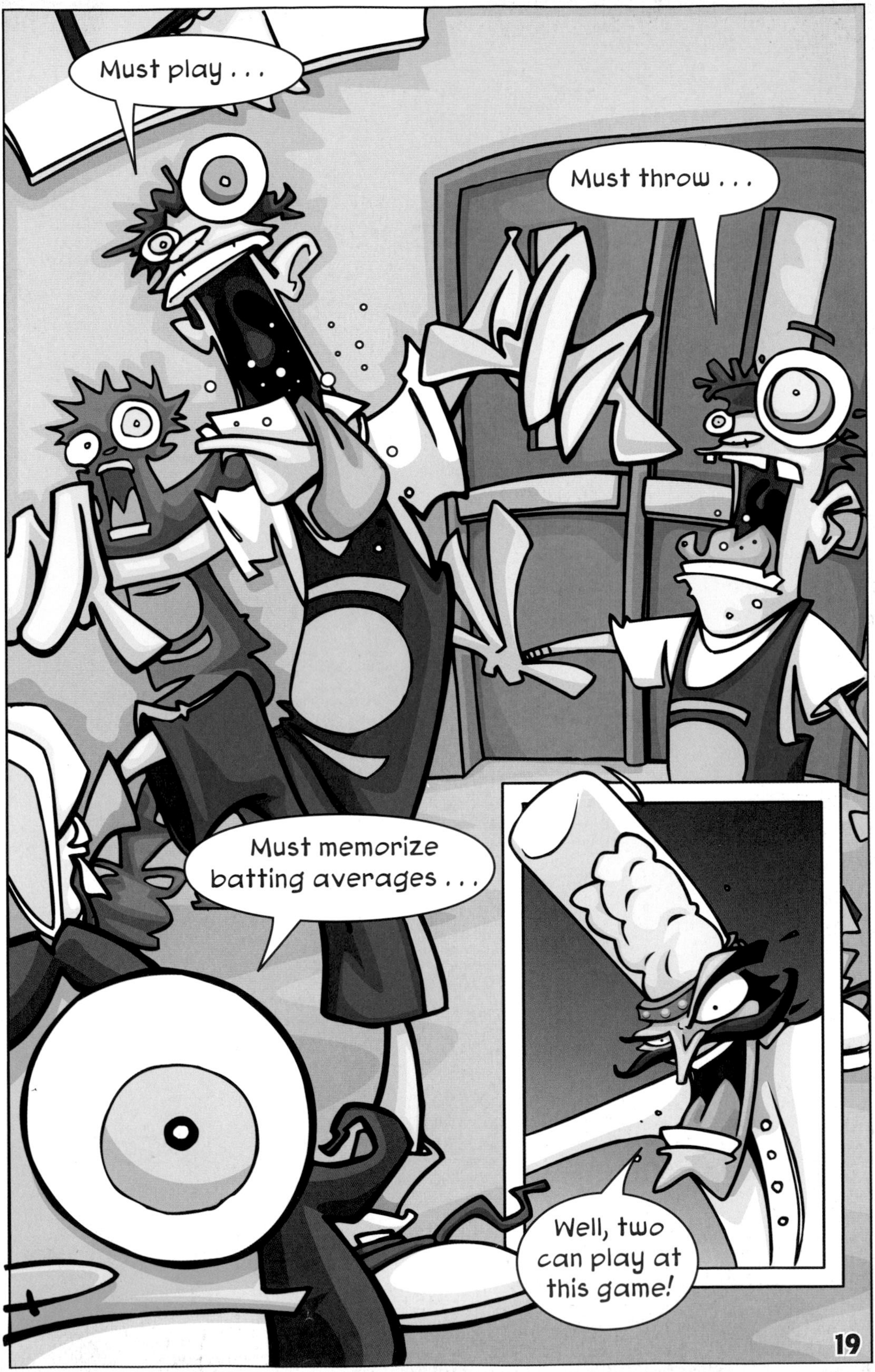

Must play . . .
Must throw . . .
Must memorize batting averages . . .
Well, two can play at this game!

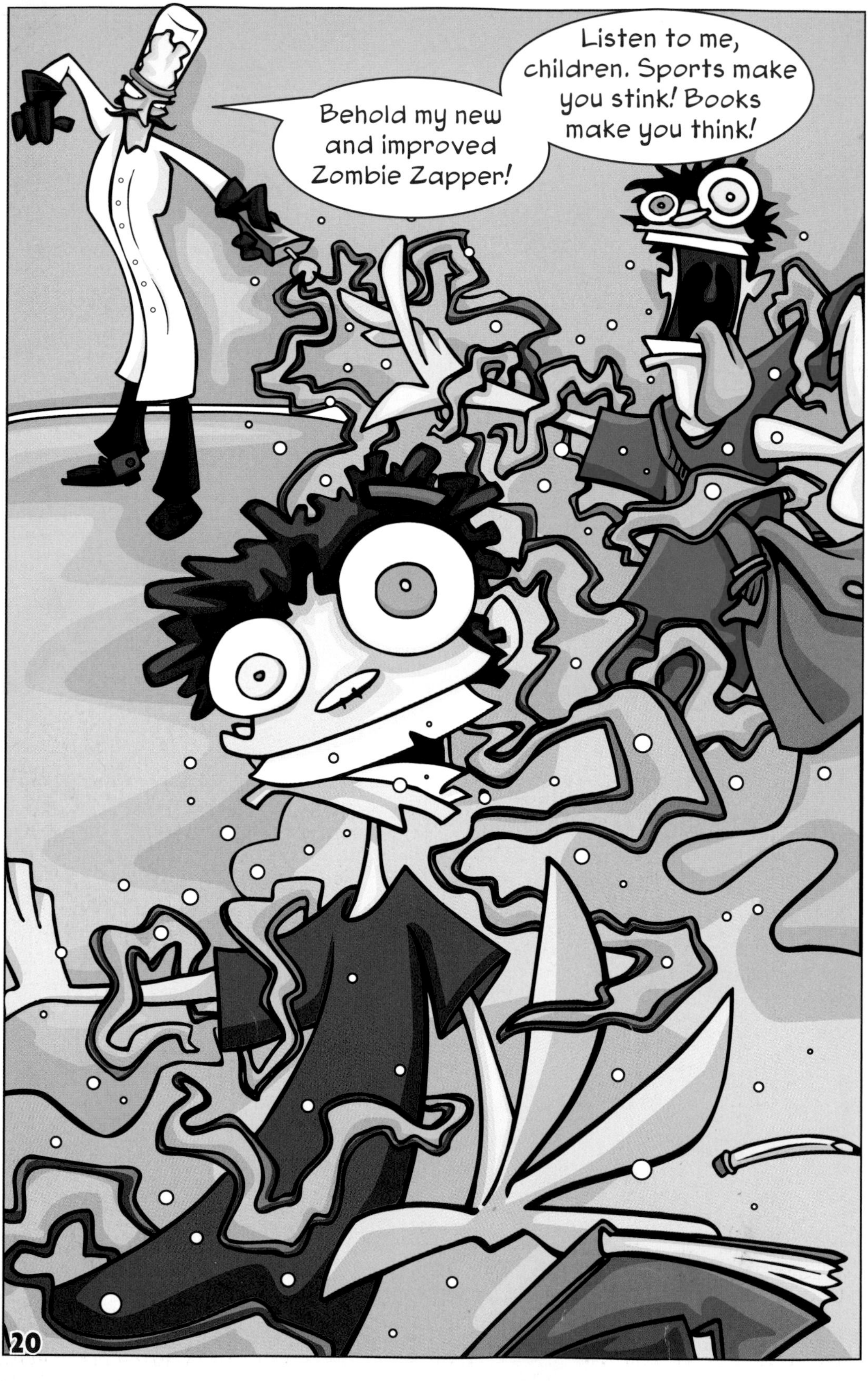
Behold my new and improved Zombie Zapper!
Listen to me, children. Sports make you stink! Books make you think!

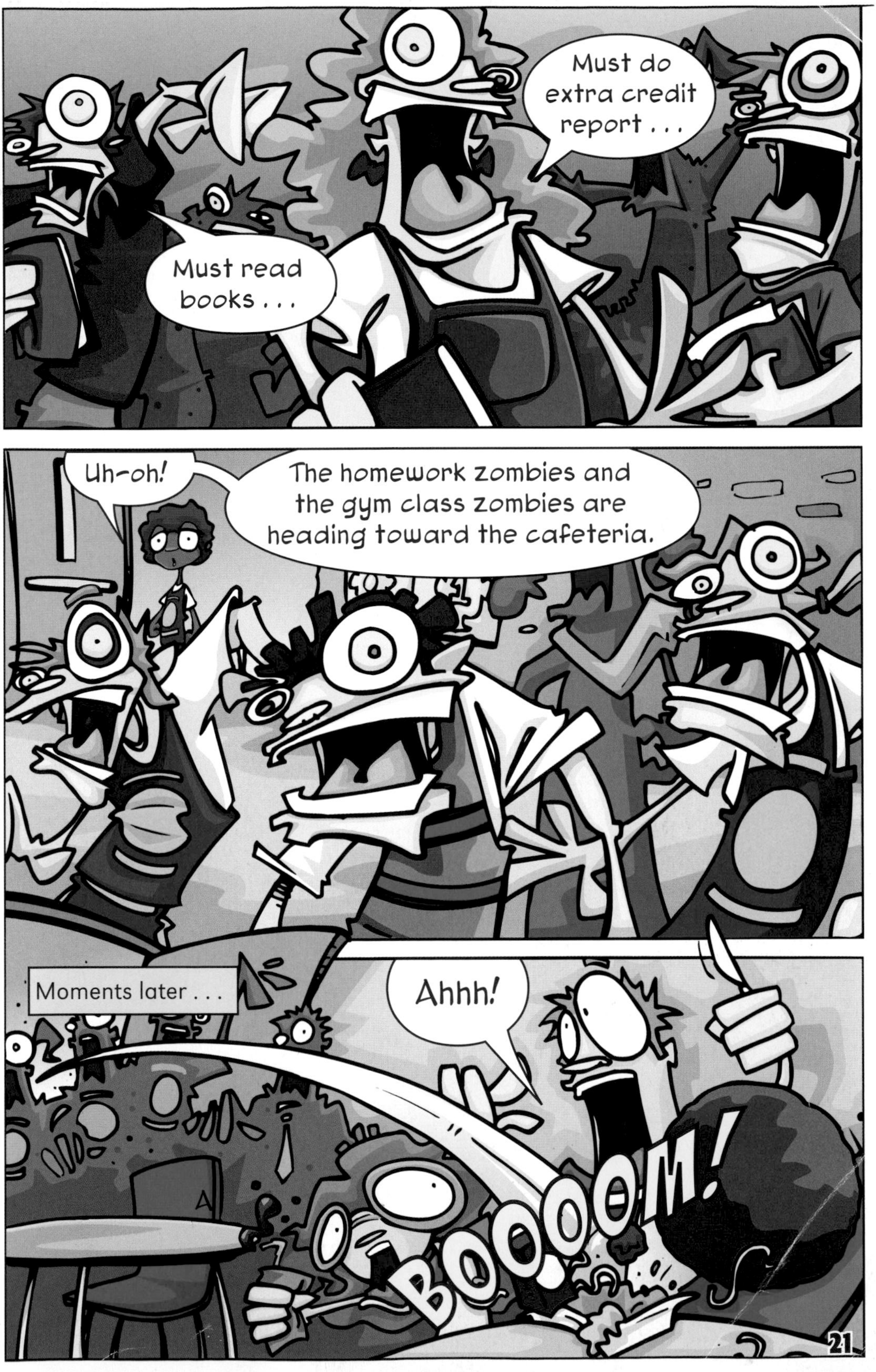
Must do extra credit report . . .
Must read books . . .
Uh-oh!
The homework zombies and the gym class zombies are heading toward the cafeteria.
Moments later . . .
Ahhh!
BOOOOOM!

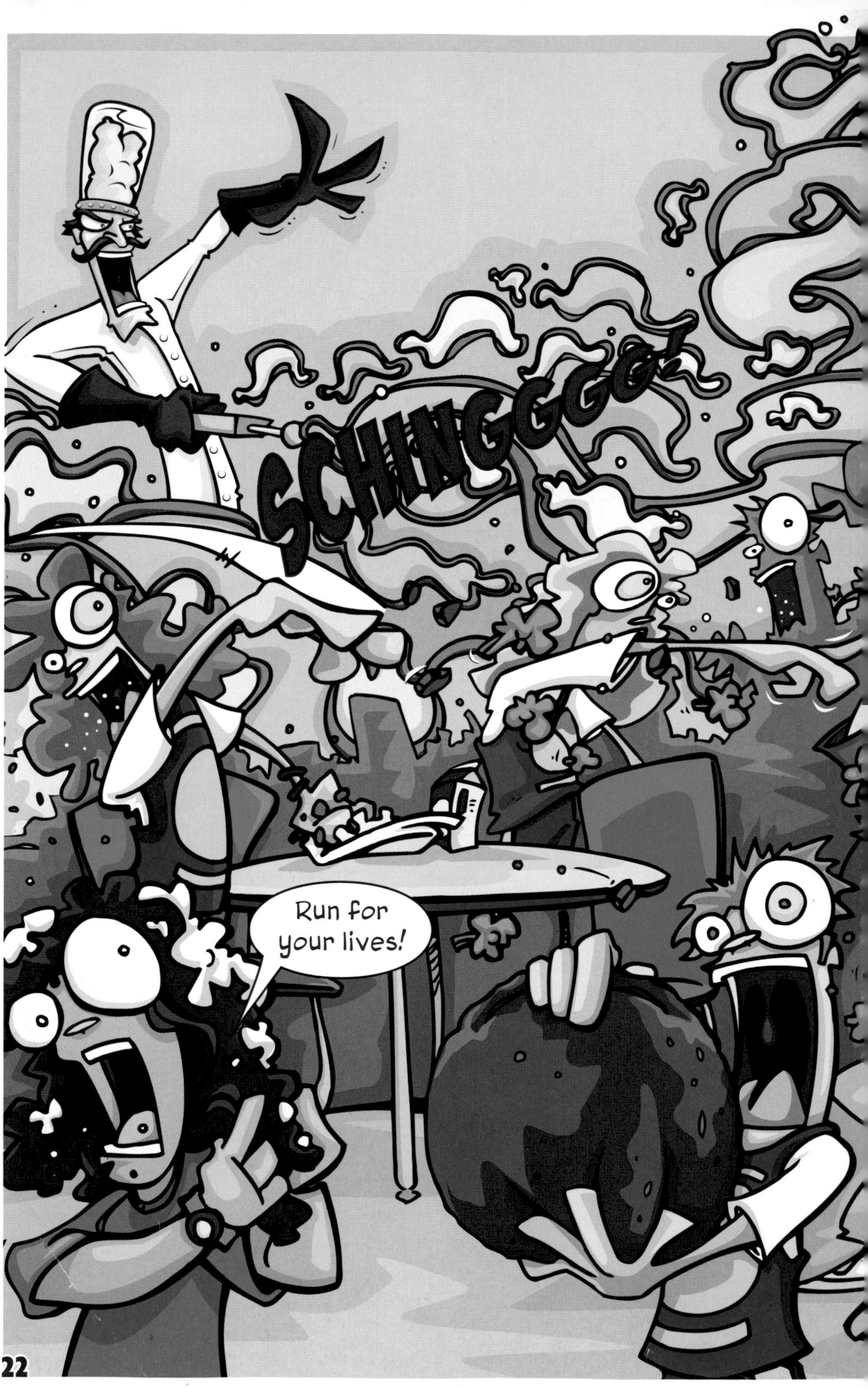
SCHINGGGGG!
Run for your lives!

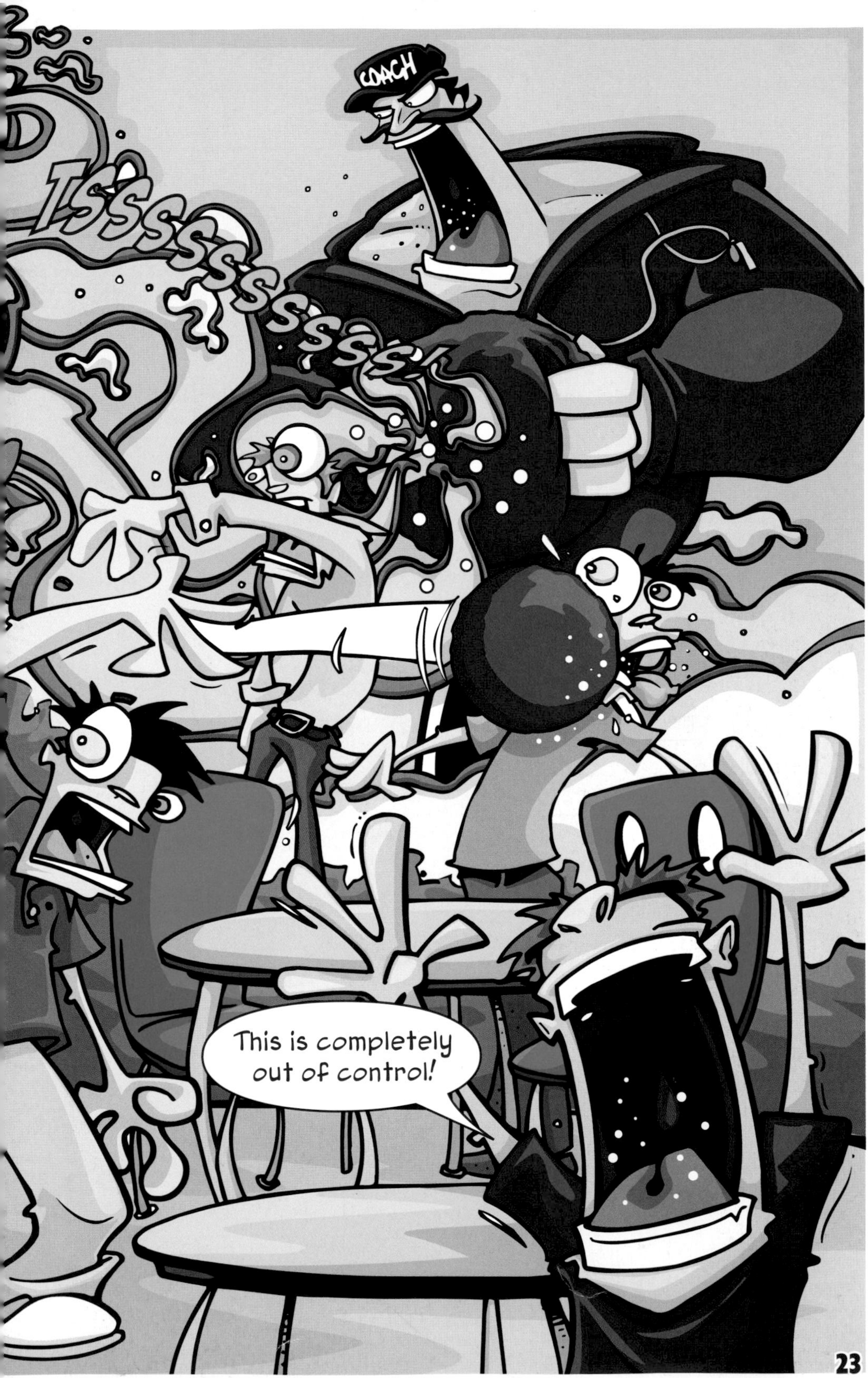
COACH
TSSSSSSSSSSS!
This is completely out of control!

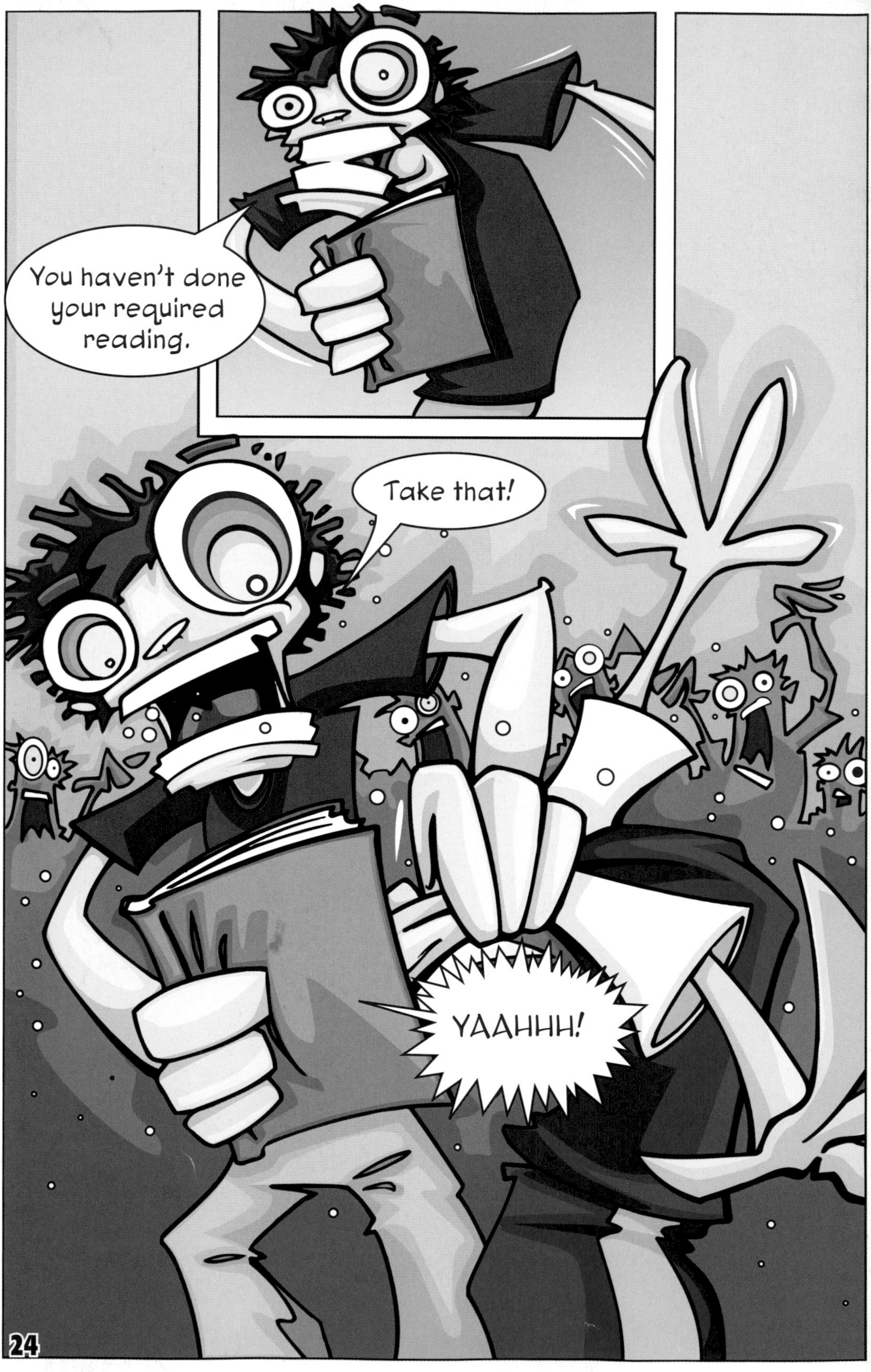
You haven't done your required reading.
Take that!
YAAHHH!

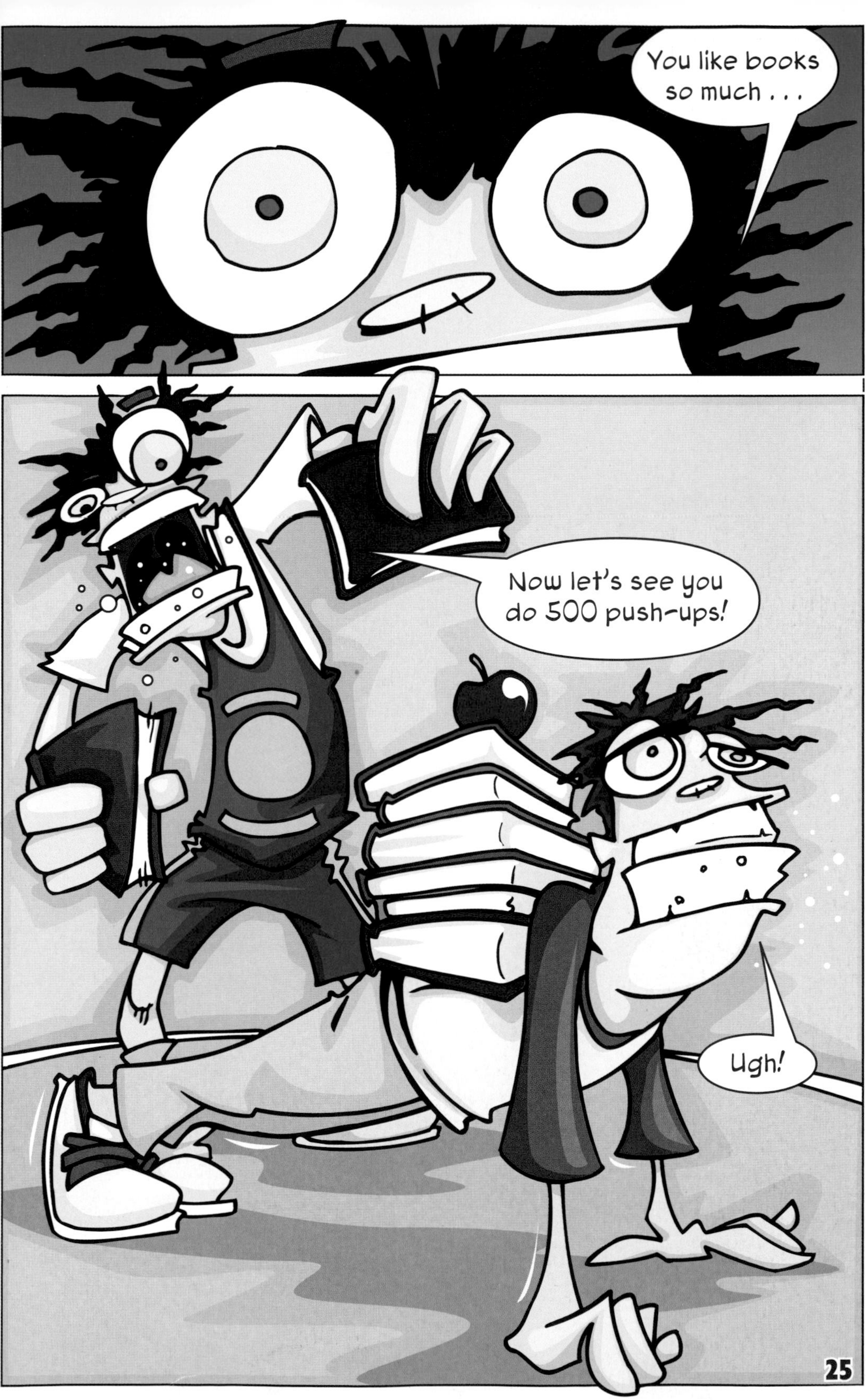
You like books so much . . .
Now let's see you do 500 push-ups!
Ugh!

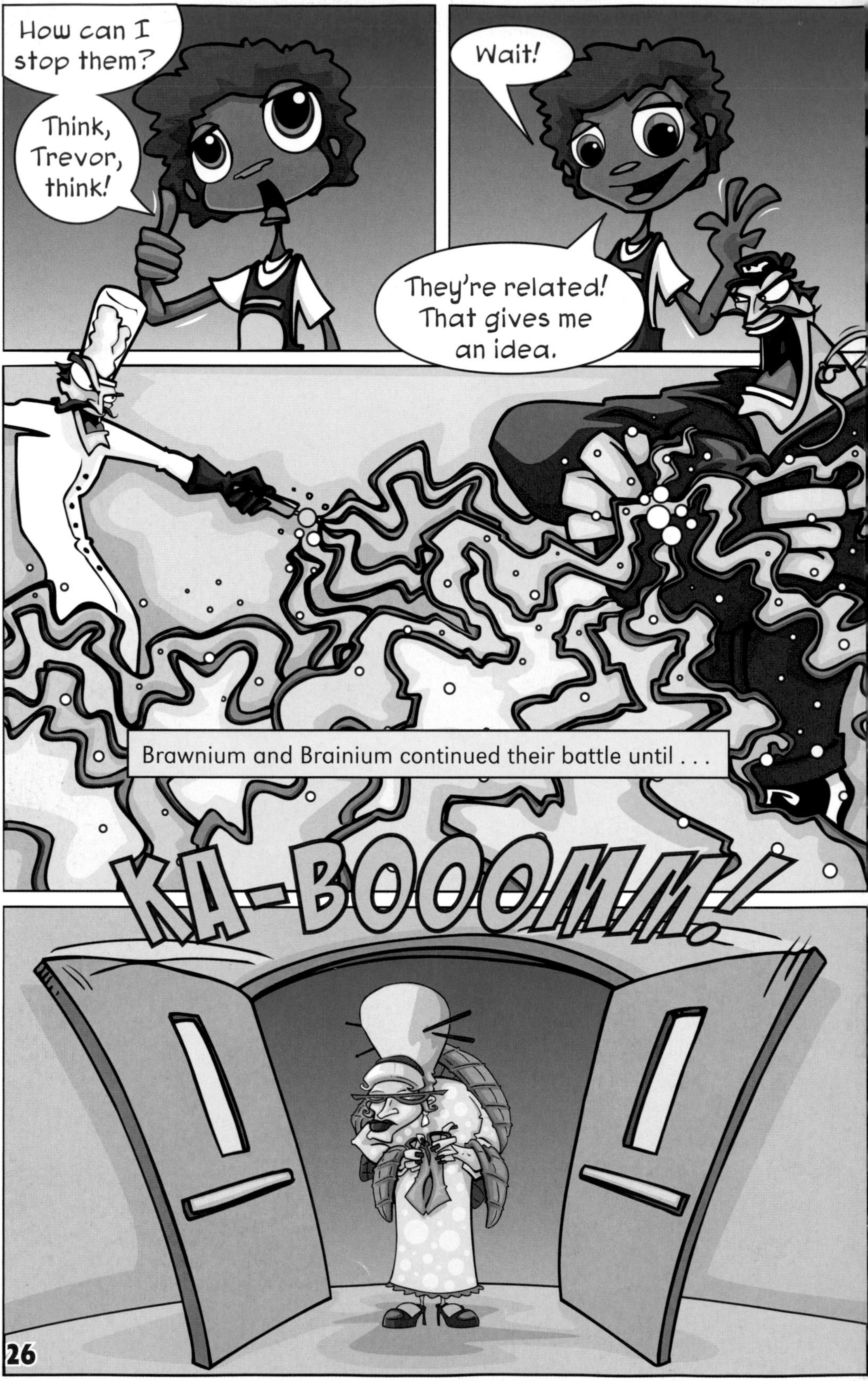
How can I stop them?
Think, Trevor, think!
Wait!
They're related! That gives me an idea.
Brawnium and Brainium continued their battle until . . .
KA-BOOOMM!

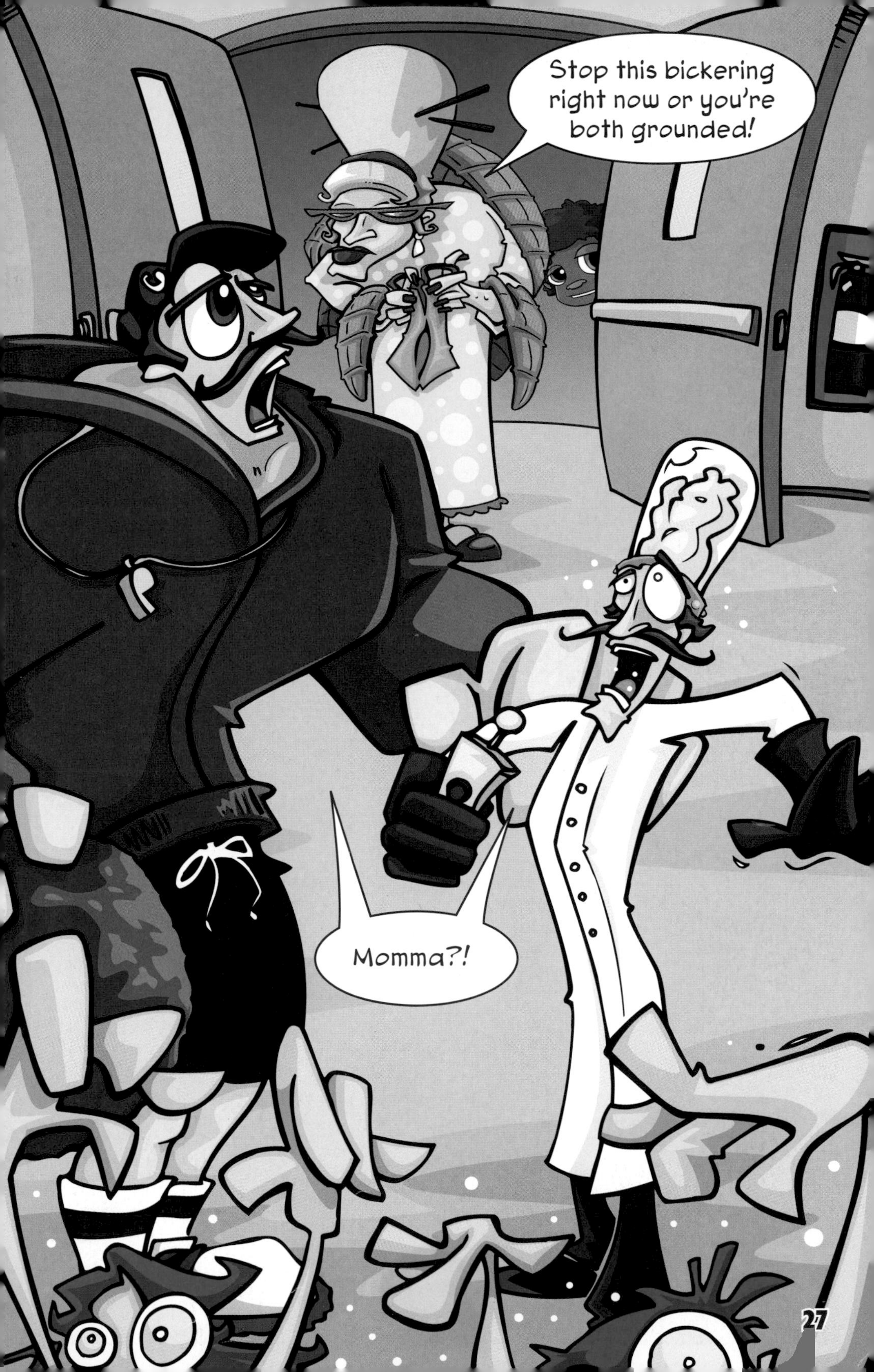
Stop this bickering right now or you're both grounded!
Momma?!

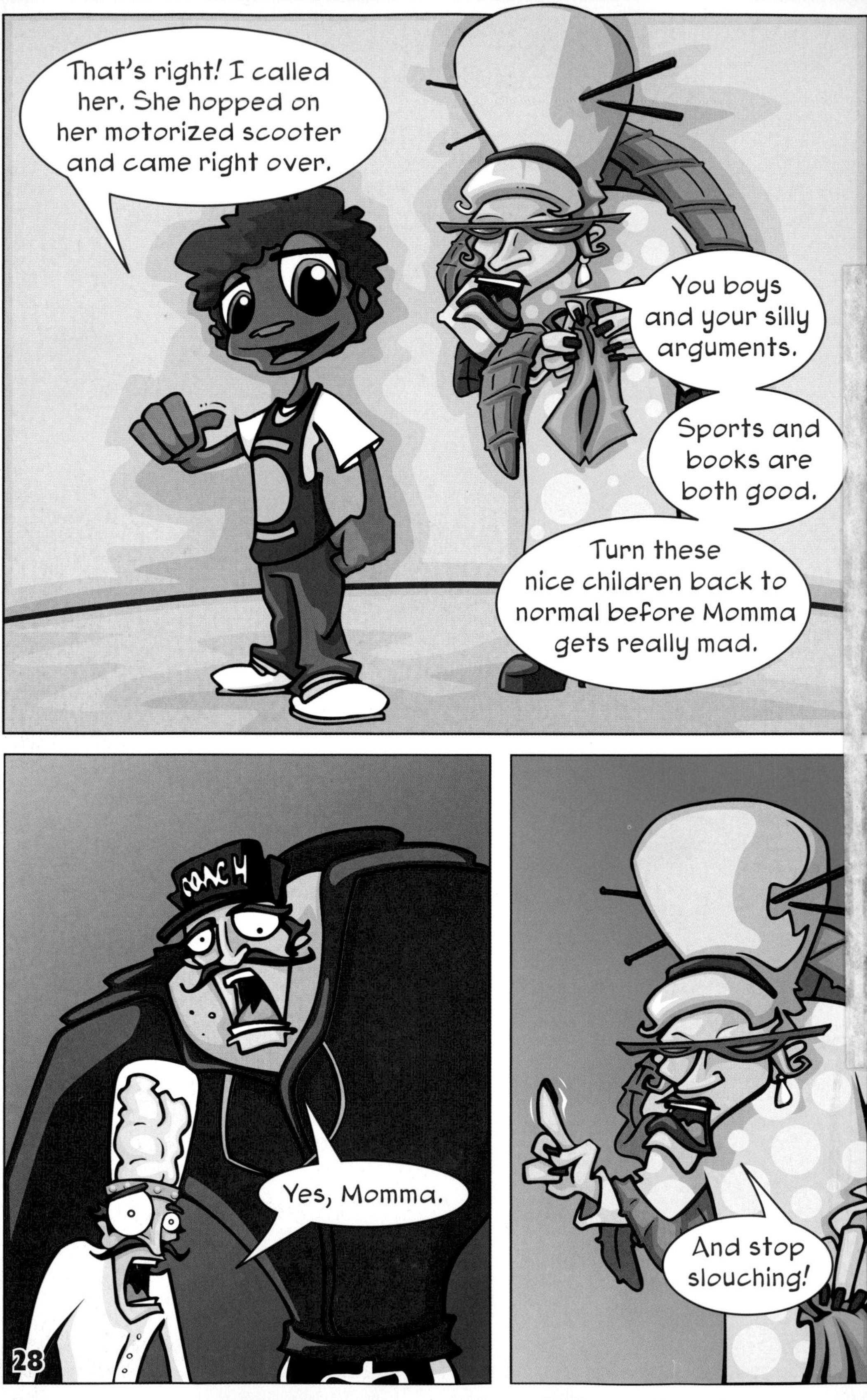
That's right! I called her. She hopped on her motorized scooter and came right over.
You boys and your silly arguments.
Sports and books are both good.
Turn these nice children back to normal before Momma gets really mad.
Yes, Momma.
And stop slouching!

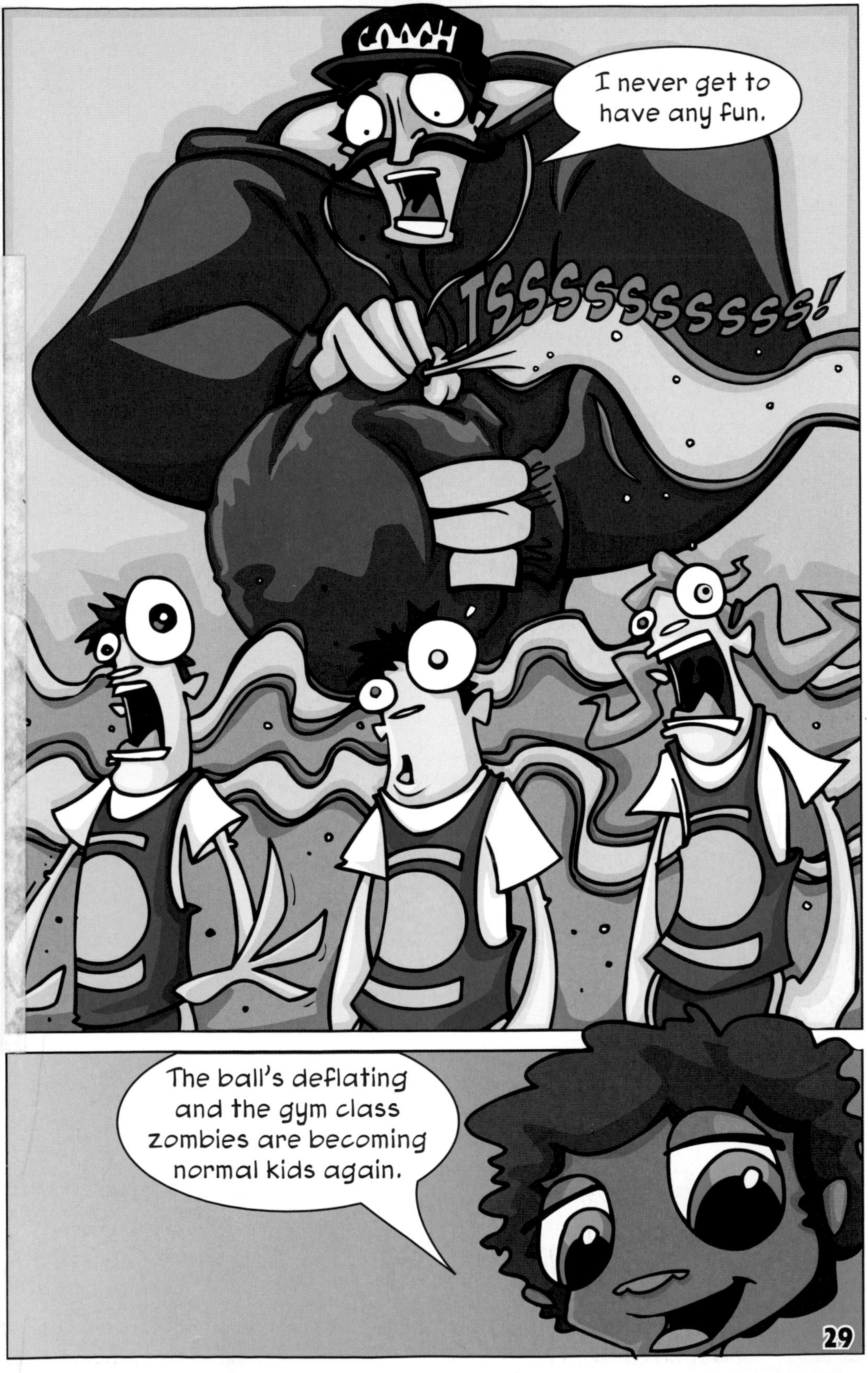
COACH
I never get to have any fun.
TSSSSSSSSSS!
The ball's deflating and the gym class zombies are becoming normal kids again.

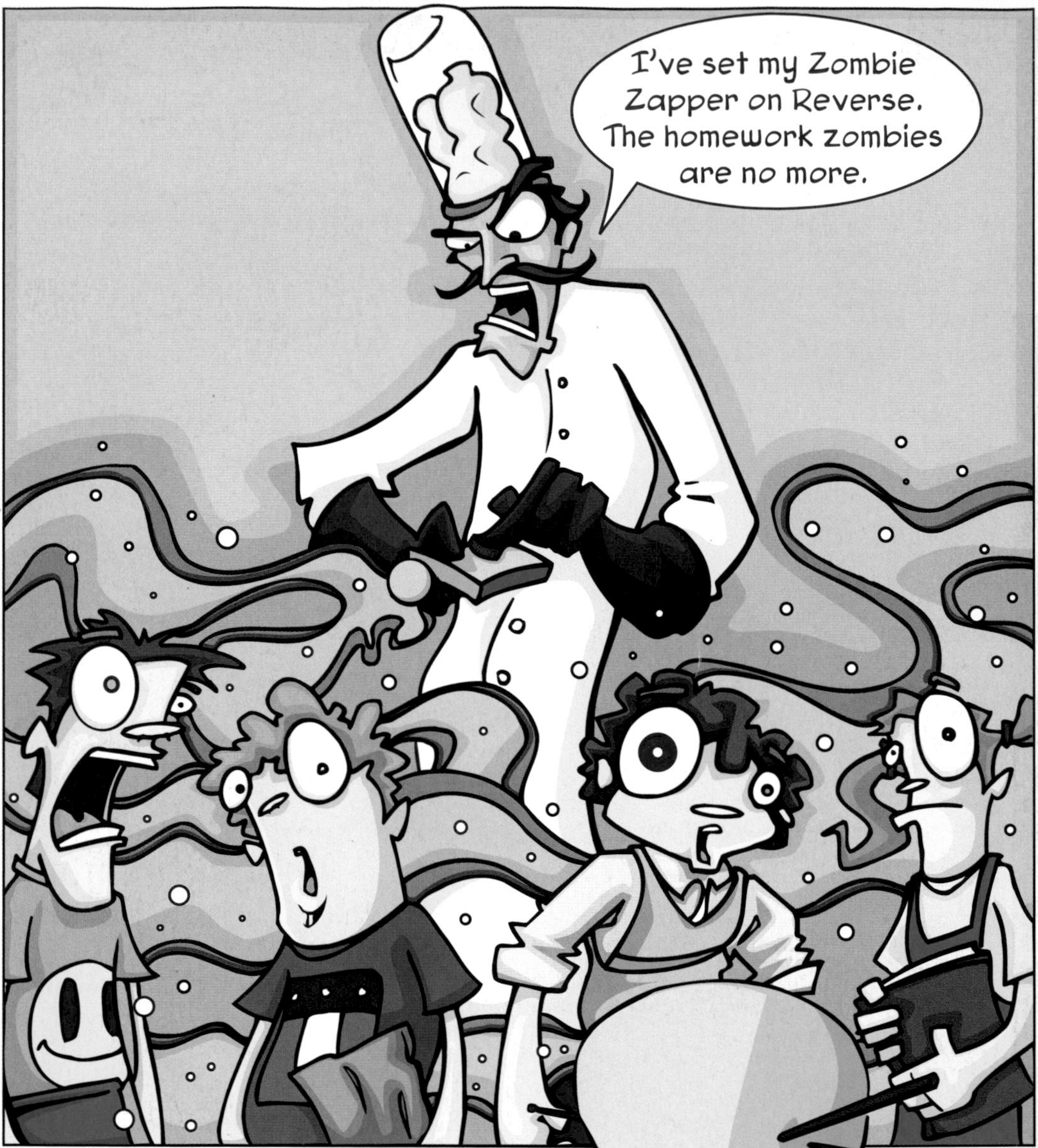
I've set my Zombie Zapper on Reverse. The homework zombies are no more.

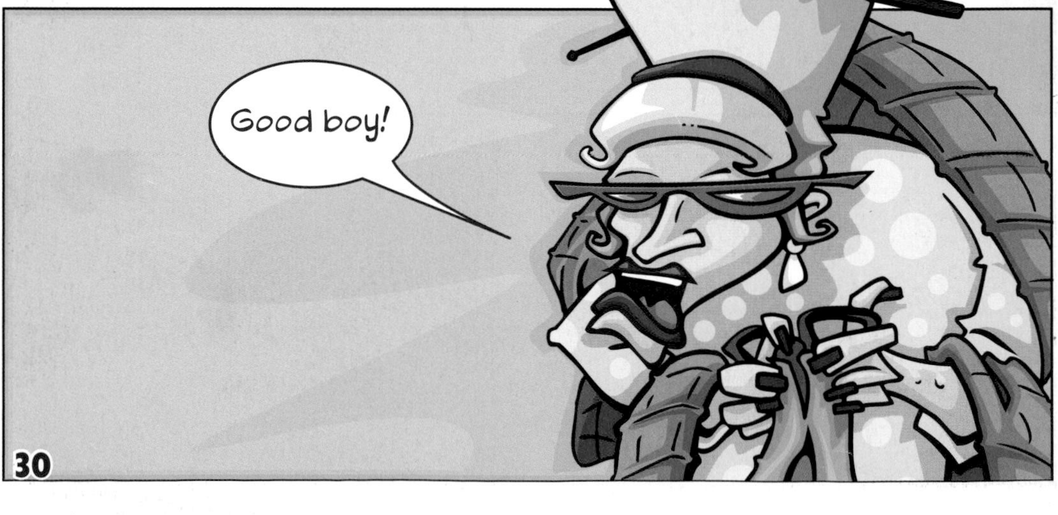
Good boy!

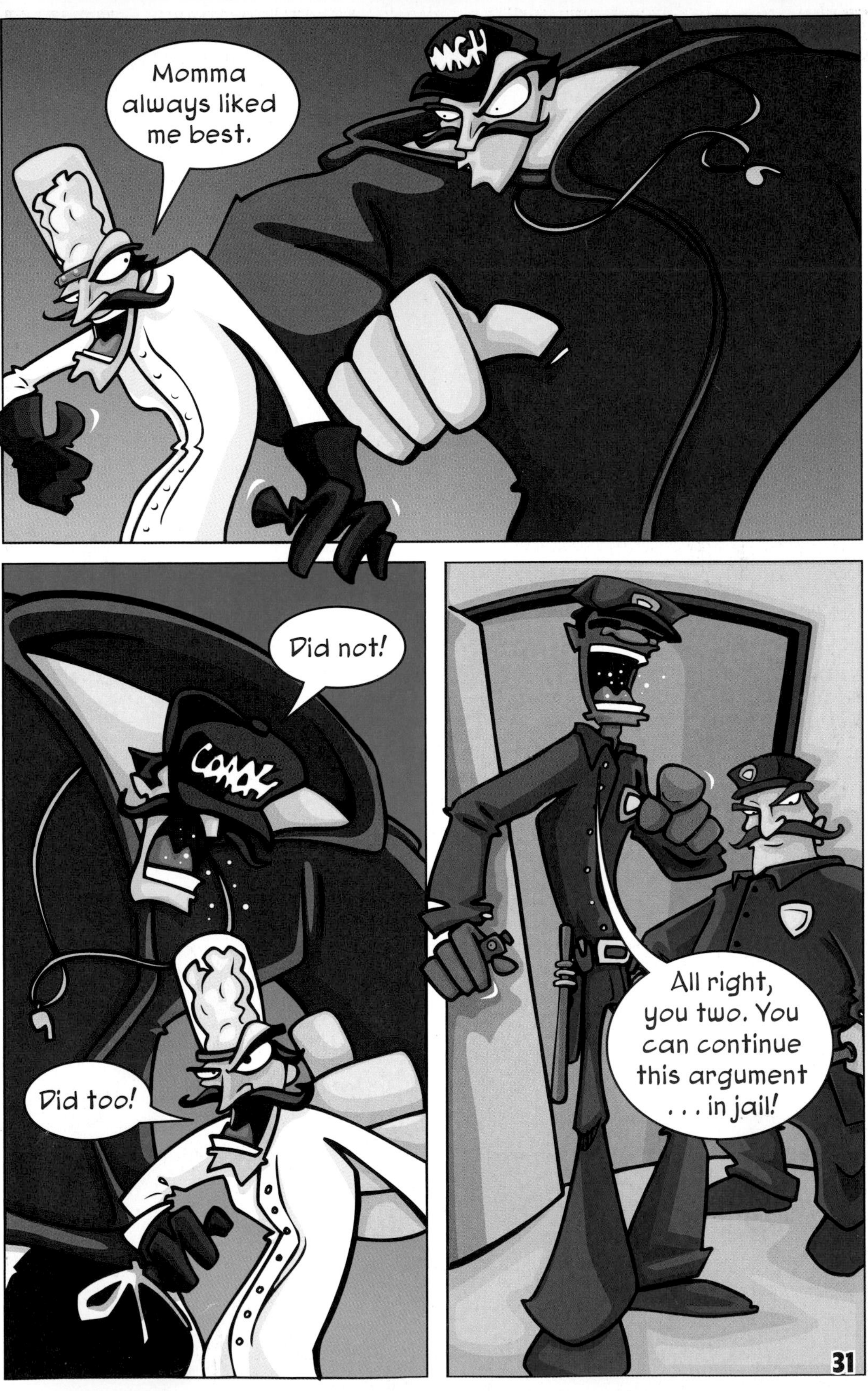
Momma always liked me best.
Did not!
Did too!
All right, you two. You can continue this argument . . . in jail!

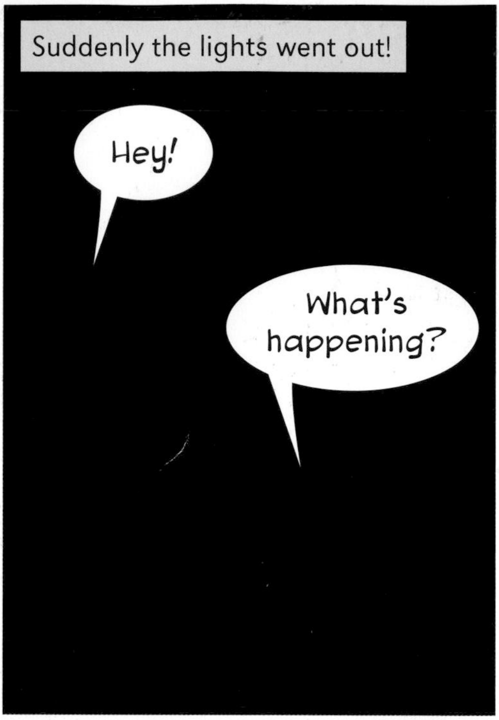
Suddenly the lights went out!
Hey!
What's happening?

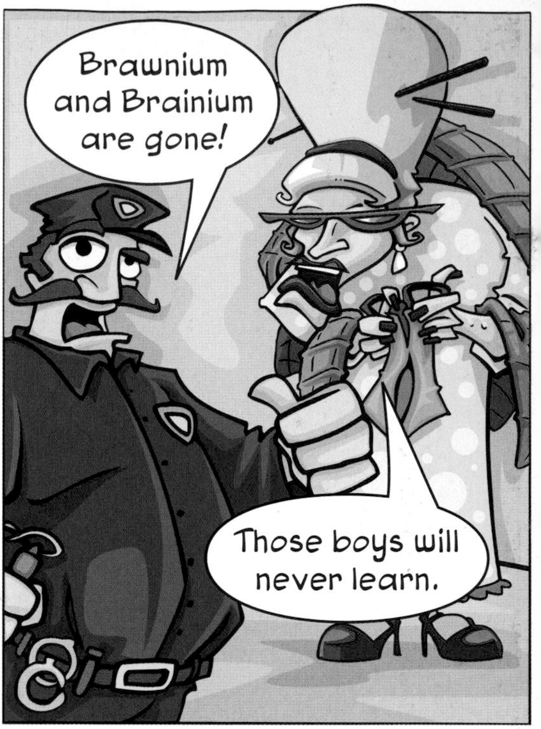
Brawnium and Brainium are gone!
Those boys will never learn.

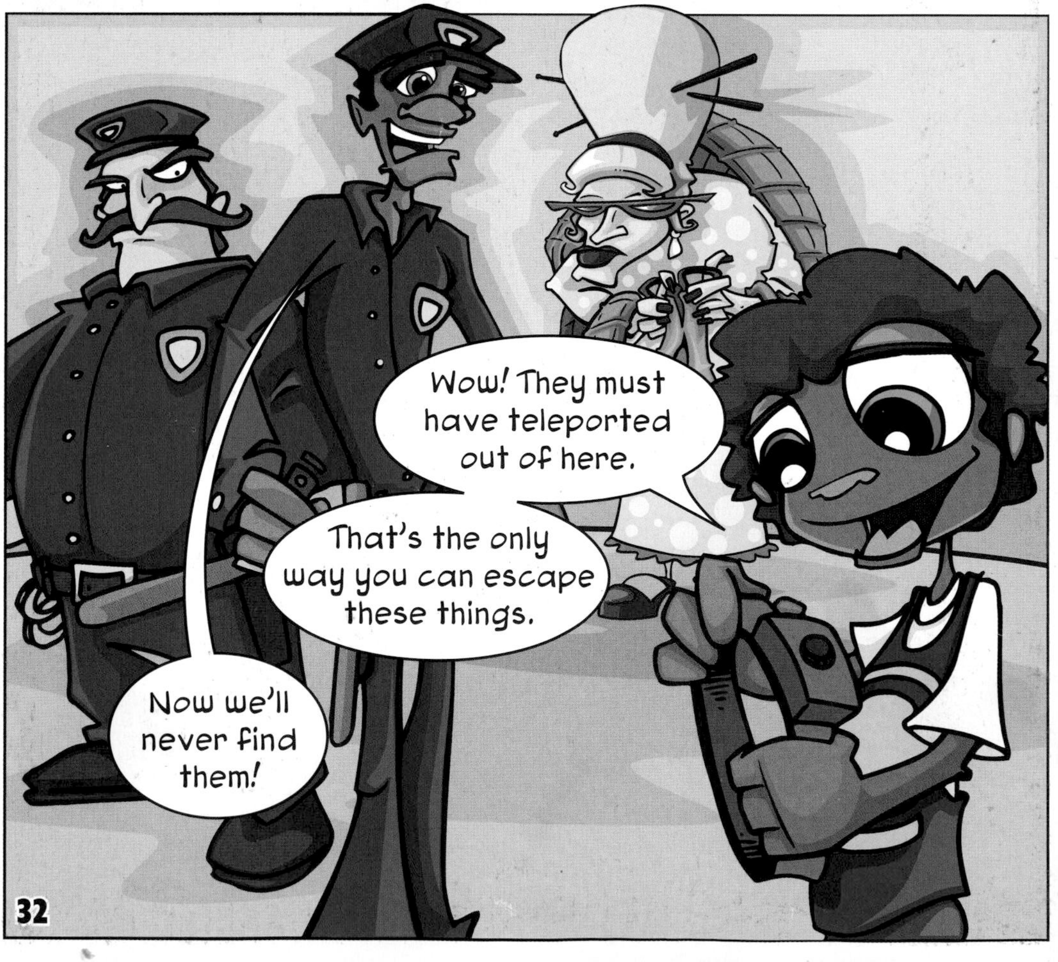
Wow! They must have teleported out of here.
That's the only way you can escape these things.
Now we'll never find them!

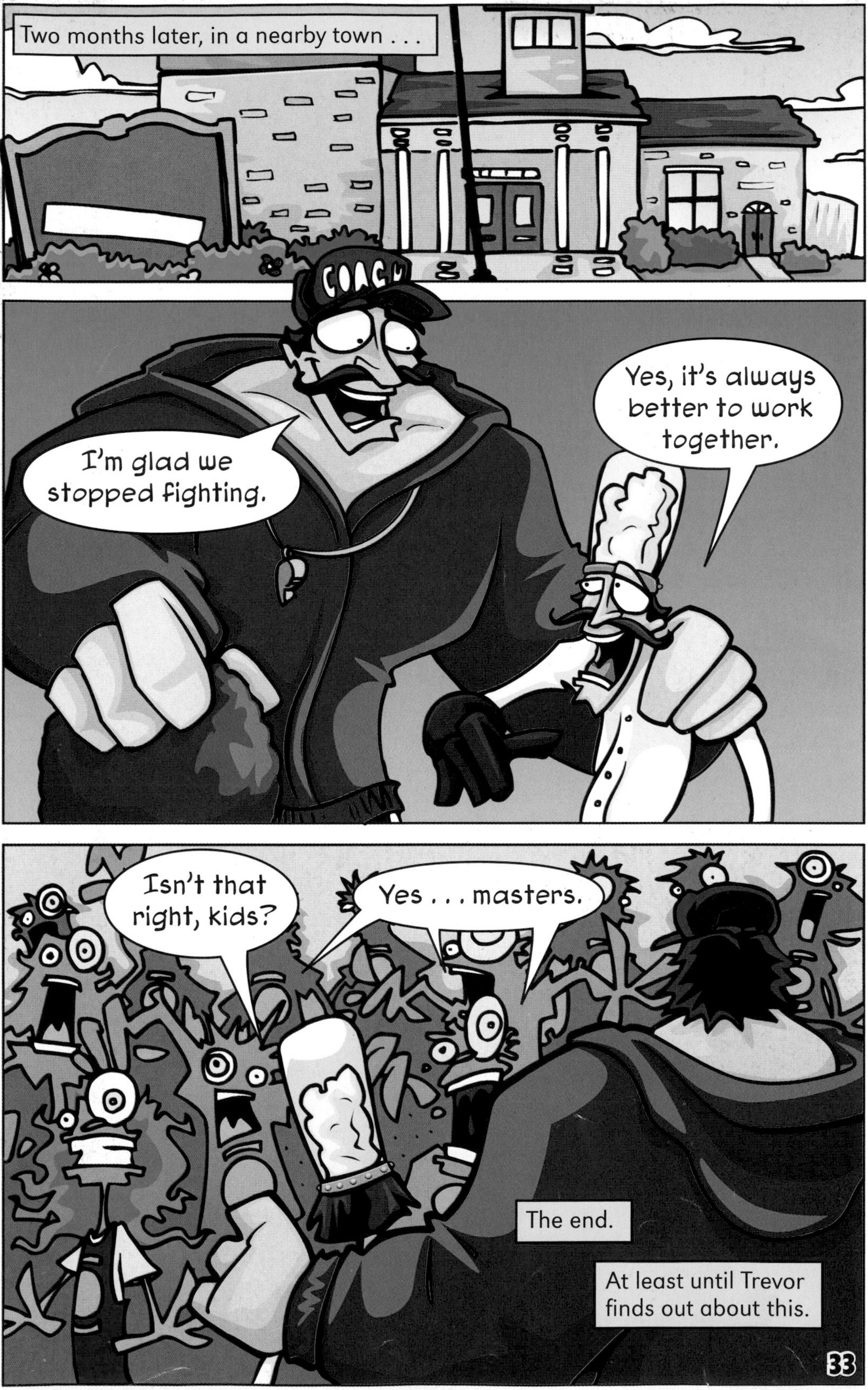

Two months later, in a nearby town . . .
COACH
I'm glad we stopped fighting.
Yes, it's always better to work together.
Isn't that right, kids?
Yes . . . masters.
The end.
At least until Trevor finds out about this.

ABOUT THE AUTHOR

Growing up, Scott Nickel wanted to be a comic book writer or a mad scientist. As an adult, he gets to do both. In his secret literary lab, Scott has created more than a dozen graphic novels for Stone Arch Books featuring time travel, zombies, robots, giant insects, and mutant lunch ladies. Scott's *Night of the Homework Zombies* received the 2007 Golden Duck award for Best Science Fiction Picture Book. When not creating crazy comics, Scott squeezes in a full-time job as a writer and editor at Jim Davis's Garfield studio. He lives in Muncie, Indiana, with his wife, two teenage sons, and an ever-growing number of cats.

ABOUT THE ILLUSTRATOR

Matt Luxich started drawing at three years old. Although his parents didn't enjoy cleaning their son's cartoons off of the walls, they supported his talent. Years later, Luxich attended the Kubert School of Illustration and Animation in Dover, New Jersey. Today, he uses the skills he learned at school in his job as a freelance illustrated and designer, working for clients such as Golden Books and the Salvation Army. When he's not drawing, Luxich likes to eat cheese slices, play with toy robots, and walk his English Bulldog, Dover.

GLOSSARY

ankle tracker (ANG-kuhl TRAK-ur)—a device attached to the ankle of some criminals, so police can locate them

brawn (BRAHN)—full of strong muscles, just like Mr. Brawnium

diaper (DYE-pur)—underwear worn by babies to protect against, um, "accidents"

pacifier (PASS-uh-fye-ur)—something for babies to suck on when they are crying

professional (pruh-FESH-uh-nuhl)—someone good enough at an activity to make it a career; major league baseball players are professional sports stars.

slouching (SLOUCH-ing)—sitting or standing with your shoulders or head drooping down

super-villain (SOOP-ur VIL-uhn)—a really evil person. Dr. Brainium isn't just a villain — he's a super villain.

teleported (TEL-uh-pohr-tud)—moved from place to place by suddenly disappearing and then reappearing somewhere else (you know, like they do in Star Trek)

tuna casserole (TOON-uh KASS-uh-role)—a meal made with tuna, noodles, mayo, and whatever else is in the cupboard

zombie (ZOM-bee)—someone whose brain is controlled by another person; when you tell your friend to eat worms, and he does it, he is acting like a zombie.

MORE ABOUT BRAINS AND BRAWN

Brains

The average brain of an adult human weighs three pounds. That's about the size of a small melon.

About 75 % of the brain is water!

Nearly 20% of the blood that flows through a human heart is pumped to the brain. The brain also uses about 20% of the air that a human breathes.

Did you know the human brain does not sense any pain? That's why brain doctors, called neurosurgeons, can operate while their patients are still awake.

Brawn

The human body has more than 600 muscles!

The largest muscle in the body is called the **gluteus maximus** (GLOO-tee-uhs MACK-sih-muhs). But it's really just a fancy word for your rear end.

The heart, also called the cardiac muscle, is a twitch muscle. These types of muscles work without you even thinking about them.

Brains and brawn have something in common. They both need exercise to get bigger, stronger, and smarter.

DISCUSSION QUESTIONS

1. What are your favorite and least favorite games to play in gym class? Explain your answer.

2. Would you rather have a super brain like Dr. Brainium or be super strong like Mr. Brawnium? Explain why you would choose one rather than the other.

3. Dr. Brainium and Mr. Brawnium are related, but they're completely different. Are your brothers, sisters, or friends different from you? Do you think it's good or bad to be different?

WRITING PROMPTS

1. Imagine you are the author, and write a story about Dr. Brainium and Mr. Brawnium when they were kids. Which brother is older? Did they like each other when they were young? Did they share their toys?

2. Make up your own gym class game! Write down the rules, make a list of the equipment each player needs, and give your game a name. Then, play your new game with friends.

3. At the end of the story, Dr. Brainium and Mr. Brawnium have turned another class into zombies. Write a story about how you would stop them once and for all.

INTERNET SITES

The book may be over, but the adventure is just beginning.

Do you want to read more about the subjects or ideas in this book? Want to play cool games or watch videos about the authors who write these books? Then go to FactHound. At *www.facthound.com*, you'll be able to do all that, and more. The FactHound website can also send you to other safe Internet sites.

Check it out!